All Men Want to Know

All Men Want to Know

NINA BOURAOUI

Translated by
Aneesa Abbas Higgins

VIKING
an imprint of
PENGUIN BOOKS

VIKING

UK | USA | Canada | Ireland | Australia
India | New Zealand | South Africa

Viking is part of the Penguin Random House group of companies
whose addresses can be found at global.penguinrandomhouse.com.

First published in France as *Tous les hommes désirent naturellement savoir* by Jean-Claude Lattès 2018
First published in Great Britain as *All Men Want to Know* by Viking 2020
001

Set in 12/14.75pt Dante MT Std
Typeset by Jouve (UK), Milton Keynes
Printed and bound in Great Britain by Clays Ltd, Elcograf S.p.A.

A CIP catalogue record for this book is available from the British Library

ISBN: 978–0–241–44772–7

www.greenpenguin.co.uk

MIX
Paper from
responsible sources
FSC® C018179

Penguin Random House is committed to a
sustainable future for our business, our readers
and our planet. This book is made from Forest
Stewardship Council® certified paper.

For my parents

'All men by nature want to know' – Aristotle, *Metaphysics*

I wonder who in this crowd is newly in love, who has just been left and who has walked out without a word, who is happy and who sad, who is fearful and who forging confidently ahead, who is hoping for a brighter future. I cross over the Seine, I walk beside nameless men and women, mirror images of me. Our hearts beat as one, we are one unit. We are alive.

I've lived in France for longer than I did in Algeria. I left Algiers on 17 July 1981, before the Black Decade. I was fourteen years old. How many friends, neighbours, acquaintances have been killed since then? I came empty-handed to Rue Saint-Charles, my first address in Paris. I stand between my two lands, two continents on either side of the sea. I cling to the flowers and brambles of my memories, photographic images that restore colour and texture to bodies bathing in the sea at Cherchell. I close my eyes, I move through Oran, Annaba, Constantine. In my mind, nothing has changed, nothing will ever change.

I could sketch the precise layout of the apartment in Algiers: the hallway and the bedrooms, the living room, the library, the streaks of light across the tiled floor I thought were messages from outer space, from other-worldly beings coming to spirit me away.

I am both architect and archaeologist.

I piece together everything I know about my family as if assembling the fragments of a shattered object. From this disorder emerges order. Silences, where echoes of the past converge. I want to know who I am, what I am made of, what I can hope for; I trace the thread of my past back as far as it will take me, making my way through the mysteries that haunt me, hoping to unravel them.

I often ask myself about the person I might have become if I'd stayed in Algeria, if I were to choose to go back there. When I say the 'person', I'm thinking of who I am in matters of love.

I search for evidence in my past, vestiges of my homosexuality, my childhood set on this path, like an asteroid circling the earth or a stream flowing down a mountain.

Paris opens itself up to me. Rue du Vieux Colombier, the Katmandou, a women-only club in the 1980s, a theatre now. The scene of many tears and fights. Where I learned the lessons of violence and submission. I close my eyes and the landscape of those nights rises up before me. I reach out and take the hand of the woman I was then. My younger self, wellspring and herald of who I am, is not lost to me.

Becoming

At the Kat, I'm eighteen years old and I don't look it. I live in Rue Notre-Dame-des-Champs, alone. My parents are stationed in one of the Emirates of the Persian Gulf. When I think of them, I see them through a veil of mist, busily going about their lives, a life that is no longer mine. I imagine them in their house, sand all around them, a long way from the centre of town, the desert encroaching on them. When the wind is high, my mother claims she can hear the helicopters and tanks from Kuwait City. I don't know if she's imagining it or alluding to a war as real as the one I'm waging against myself.

My first time at the Kat, I'm asked to show ID, then I become one of the regulars. I go there on Fridays, Saturdays, Tuesdays and sometimes Thursdays. On weeknights, the emptiness of the place intensifies my loneliness. My fantasies are of murder and torture. The price I believe I must pay for being who I am.

Tables in the golden square, nearest to the bar, are reserved for actresses and girls from the escort agency with the men they bring in. Men who observe from the sidelines, stealing glances at the slow-dancing women, keeping their distance, that's the rule. I look around for a hand to lead me across the field of bodies, all of them unknown to me but sharing my desire: to be loved.

The women at the Kat scare me, they're different from me, from the women of my childhood; these women bury their softness beneath layers of anger so it won't be exposed, vulnerable. The night is destructive – perhaps it will destroy me in turn.

I'm afraid I'll run into one of them as I walk along Boulevard Saint-Germain and down Rue de Rennes, as I approach the door of this place that's drawing me in, the place I leave in the small hours to walk home, skirting the boundary fence of the Jardin du Luxembourg.

I pray to the trees, the statues, the fountains, put my faith in the power of all this beauty watching over me. I'm leading a double life, following a path that's strewn with thorns and nettles. I don't know where it will lead me.

Remembering

In Algiers, all that separates the gardens of our building from the eucalyptus forest are strips of barbed wire; it's easy to prise them apart and slip into the forest.

The trees thrust like swords towards the sun. Night falls on my skin; I feel the earth beating under my hand, beneath my belly as I lie down. I smell its perfume of amber and resin. The earth is a body, a maze of nerves and blood vessels.

They say that men come here to lie together in the fallen leaves. Men from the city, from the docks usually. They make their way one by one, strangers who meet and embrace, safe from watching eyes. People say they leave a part of themselves in this earth, that the soil has become more fertile. These men seem to me to exist on a higher plane. In my dreams I become them, I cast aside the feminine part of my being, the part that doesn't chime with my desires, with the paths I take. I cleave to their hands, their breath. I am no longer a daughter. I will never be a wife. I am the child of these men who lie in the forest.

Becoming

At first, I go alone to the Kat. I don't have any lesbian friends, I don't want any. I avoid all connections beyond the club itself. I don't give out my phone number, I go by a false name, create an identity for myself, a hologram that fades away as quickly as it comes together; I'd wipe away my fingerprints if I could.

I become paranoid, I have a recurring dream of a voice calling me on the phone and saying: 'I know who you are, I know who you are.' I'm terrified at the thought of being unmasked, of being found deserving of punishment.

I pay cash to get in, buy my drinks with cash, don't use my credit card or my chequebook, and when I run out of money I go out to the cash machine and come straight back.

I don't carry a handbag, I keep everything in my jacket pocket. I wear a jacket even when it's not cold and I never leave it in the cloakroom, that way I can make a quick getaway if there's a fight or if the police are called.

Remembering

I haven't forgotten my roots: the cliffs of the corniche, the palm grove of Bou Saada, the walking trails of Chréa, the reeds along the seashore, the medlar trees I used to climb, hauling myself up above the world, my teeth tearing into the fruit hanging from the branches, flooding me with a pleasure I never tired of seeking.

I remember the road from the Place d'Hydra to our apartment block built by Shell in the 1950s for the French oil workers of Total.

I remember the houses, the steep streets, the bends in the roads, the widest one in front of the French Embassy, the guard's sentry box, the concrete blocks of the car parks, the lift cabin gliding over a dark-green wall as it rises, the fake marble staircase, the wrought-iron balustrade, the tiled floor with carpets laid over it, the curving lines of the buildings set out in rows in order of size in the manner of Le Corbusier.

I can no longer recall the names of the streets, French names Arabized in the 1980s, nor the names of our neighbours or of the families that lived close by. But the shapes, colours, textures, all the details of the decor are still with me; a stage empty of actors, a city of ghosts.

In Algiers, my family seems to me to be one living being, whole and unique. We have no need of others, we are enough as we are, my sister in her bedroom, my mother on the balcony, the cat at her feet, my father filing his papers. Everything is in its place: furniture, objects, the people who use them.

I move through the apartment as if gazing out from within a painting on the wall, from the tapestry that hangs in the living room, images of voluptuous women on a riverbank, cherubs beside them, ferns, poplars.

I feel the happiness in my body, waves of happiness, a sensation I can pinpoint; it comes when we are all together.

It cannot be real, such happiness, it cannot endure. There will be a price to pay for it.

Becoming

I begin to write when I first start going to the Kat.

My night-time outings are inner dramas. I go out alone, as a man would, believing myself to be free. But this is no freedom: no one's waiting for me, no one's hoping I'll be there. I'm nothing. I know it and I'm ashamed.

Sitting at the bar, I wait. It's sad but I accept it – I don't like it here but this place has something I'm searching for. Every night the same songs, nothing changes from one evening to the next; it reminds me of death. I watch the women dancing together and the only thing that shocks me is how alone I am.

Words are the balm for my nights spent in search of something that eludes me, in search of love, of beauty remembered – women reclining on the rocks, my mother's and sister's voices calling me from the sixth floor of the apartment block in Algiers, a lightness sometimes: the days we spent away from the city and its web of fears, playing in the creeks, on the rocks.

When I begin to write, my first creation is a woman, alone and abused. I don't realize I'm sketching a portrait of my mother.

Remembering

My mother comes into our apartment in Algiers, her dress torn, drops of spit in her hair, her skin streaked with grime, clutching her hands to her breasts as if to hide them. She doesn't cry, she makes her way to the bathroom, asks us not to follow her. I pick up her shoes and bag thrown down in the hallway. I go to my room and wait for her, my sister comes to join me; I make a paper aeroplane, launch it at the wall.

We carry on as if nothing has happened. My mother washes herself, she takes her time, she scrubs her body to rub away the imprints of the fingers that have touched her. Then she says: 'I was attacked by a madman. I managed to get away. I took cover in a shop. I think he tried to strangle a child too, although I'm not absolutely sure.'

I open all the windows in the apartment, fear flies out, the beauty of nature flows in and wraps itself around us: treetops, sun shining through the clouds. I pray to heaven to mend this image; this 'dirty image' I call it, because of the thoughts it gives rise to. I imagine a creature, half man, half beast, pinning my mother to the ground, devouring her. This is the dark place I come from.

Later, I will make it my duty to protect other women from danger, even when there is none.

Remembering

In Paris, our building is number 118 on Rue Saint-Charles. It's a modern five-storey building with latticework balconies. My mother chose it because of its proximity to the Boucicaut Hospital, which she finds reassuring. It has a living room with large sliding-glass windows and one bedroom with a trestle table set up as my desk.

I sleep with my mother, my bed pushed right up against hers. At night, I listen to *Boulevard de l'étrange* on the radio. My new situation in Paris seems just as weird to me as the ghost stories I'm listening to.

When we were living in Algiers, while my father was away on diplomatic missions to Washington, we used to watch an English television series called *Thriller*. We'd sleep together afterwards, all three of us, my sister, my mother and I in one bed. My mother was afraid 'they' would come after us 'with knives'.

Remembering

The Algerian terror begins for me with the death of a psychiatrist in the 1990s.

Because I know him. Because he was murdered in his consulting room in Mustapha Pasha Hospital.

His skin, his red hair, his laugh are familiar to me, his voice calling to us in the lemon grove, 'Lunch is ready, children,' as we play our game of 'chuck the ball at the wall, the ball goes over the wall, a passer-by picks it up, pockets it and walks on'. His gentleness the day I told him I'd dreamed of a wall that suddenly sprang up in front of me and came crashing down on my head.

Because I was his son's protector in the Hydra School playground.

Because his French wife wore pleated skirts and blouses of material so fine you could see her freckled skin beneath; every freckle the imprint of a kiss – a kiss from Doctor G.

Becoming

At the Kat, I experience a form of social unease, a class anxiety that fills me with shame. I'm mixing with women outside my social circle, factory workers, former prisoners, prostitutes. We are thrown together by fate, driven together by the one thing we share: our sexual orientation.

I'm a victim of my own homophobia. I despise myself for sneering at the embracing couples on the benches, the girls locked in one another's arms on the dance floor, the courageous couples in the street. I resent them for flaunting themselves in this way. I could be compromised if I were seen with them.

I envy their freedom. I stay locked into my fear. When someone offers me a lift out of concern for my safety, I refuse; they might remember my address, come to my door the next day, I could be outed to my fellow students at the university who know nothing of my 'tendencies', my 'invert' nature; I use these outmoded expressions to taunt myself and because the Kat exists outside of time, cut off from the 1980s I'm living through. I'd rather walk home, be followed; it's the price I pay for calling into existence what I call my 'nature'.

I'm not breaking any laws but I'm flirting with decadence; I must be, I spend so much time at the Kat.

Only writing is innocent. I write in complete freedom: I have no timetable, no obligations; words, phrases well up, abrupt, sudden, intrusive, only to disappear as soon as I go back out into the night.

Remembering

When my father goes away on assignment for several weeks, we're left alone with my mother in our apartment; I listen to Joe Dassin's 'L'été indien', his voice is soothing.

I'm scared of the wind in the trees, of the shadows on the walls of my room, of the visions I conjure in my mind: images that spring up unbidden, of monsters or souls in torment. I'm afraid my mother will suffocate while she sleeps and neither my sister nor I will be able to revive her, I'm afraid the man-beast will come back to harm her.

I feel guilty but I don't know how I've sinned.

Becoming

I become part of a group, Ely's group, and my nights are trans-formed. To gain acceptance, I play the part of the writer, slightly disdainful.

Ely is blonde with short hair, she wears Chanel suits, strings of pearls and Hermès scarves, and she won't dance to anything but Bibi Flash or Chagrin d'amour songs.

Ely drinks whisky, vodka, rum – anything to get drunk fast – she can't afford to waste time. She's bored; nothing really engages her, or very little, nothing surprises her any more; she sees into people's hearts and minds, she knows all about life and, at the age of twenty-five, she's already come to terms with death. She sometimes threatens to kill herself if she hasn't found true love by the end of the year. But love is something she doesn't believe in.

I feel comfortable around Ely, crazy as she is. Her voice stands out, it guides me towards her as I thread my way through the night, through the forest of women.

Remembering

My sister and I record our voices on cassette tapes. We note the contents on every tape. *Impressions*: Dalida, Sylvie Vartan, Marie Myriam at Eurovision. *Serials*: 'The Adventures of Colonel Irbicht', 'Parents Divorcing', 'Night of the Living Dead'. *Goosebumps*: wind in the trees, neighbours rowing. *Nothing*: us breathing.

We invent a life inspired by our own and act it out. As the younger sister, I play the minor characters, but my voice drowns out my sister's, flooding the soundtrack with its croaky timbre, damaged from too much shouting.

Our cassettes go missing one day, even though we keep them in a special box. I picture the person finding them, imagine them trying to guess who we are from our far-fetched stories, our voices singing above the records playing on the chrome Hitachi turntable.

The seventies are a world apart, much more than just an era. The seventies are another country, a place of no return.

Remembering

The place our mother calls our 'spot' in the Algerian country-side, the hidden footpaths, the haunted forest we venture deep into, songs of the djinns weaving through the trees, the forest from which I think we'll never return, or only come back changed, the dry riverbed, bosom of nature, where we eat our picnics, wary of approaching storms that could cause the waters to rise in an instant and drown us all.

My Algeria is a place of poetry, beyond reality. I've never been able to write about the massacres. I'm not entitled to, I can't, I'm the Frenchwoman's daughter. *Ana khayif* – I'm scared.

Becoming

Can women catch AIDS from each other, I wonder, is it transmitted by the hands, by saliva, or does it die quickly in contact with the air? No one talks about it, out of fear, ignorance, embarrassment. I keep it at the back of my mind as a threat, an imagining, something else to worry about.

I use a torch and a magnifying mirror to inspect the inside of my mouth, my skin and mucous membranes, looking for a sore, a mark; I feel my armpits, my throat.

I hunt down information on how it's transmitted, I read everything I can about it, hungrily.

In the gay community (I like these two words, they don't so much belong to me as own me) only men are affected, decimated; apart from a couple of junkies there have been no cases of gay women afflicted by this disease they call the 'gay plague'.

The truth is that women are afraid to speak out.

Knowing

My Algerian grandmother used to call my mother the 'Swede', on account of her blonde hair, her fair skin and blue eyes.

The first time she met her, she hugged her close, belly to belly, chest to chest, kissed her as she would her daughter. She stroked her face, her shoulders, her skin, told her she was beautiful, very beautiful, and what's more, she had soft skin, so important in a woman; then she asked her not to wear a bikini any more when she went to the beach with men – it wasn't done in Algeria, there are rules to be respected, relations between men and women follow strict guidelines.

My father's female cousins, seeing their hopes dashed, would happily have chopped my mother to pieces and eaten her, seasoned with salt and pepper.

When packages arrived in the post – offerings of grapes, strawberries, pastries, cut flowers – my father threw them out, to protect against evil spells. He said there were women who could place curses on people by rolling couscous grains in a dead man's hand and making gifts of the couscous.

He tore up the letters too, for other people's words are known to bring bad luck.

Becoming

I can't separate the Kat from my first urge to write, as if the body's yearnings, fulfilled or unfulfilled, provided a pathway to the world of the imagination, as if accepting and exploring a sexuality outside of the norm, discovering a new world, were a conduit to books, to words.

I construct a bridge between two worlds, the world of Rue du Vieux Colombier and the world of pens, paper, typewriters. I go back and forth ceaselessly between the two, sinking and breaking free.

I don't know which holds more danger for me, the life I'm building or the life recreated, written about, altered sometimes, improved upon.

Writing is an elixir – the act of writing soothes me, brings me happiness.

Knowing

When my mother met my father, the young French Muslim – as Algerians were referred to before 1962 – studying law and economics at the University of Rennes, she was dubbed 'Khadija, the Arab' by the other students.

When she told her parents about him, she was suddenly cast as the interloper and ordered to leave the family home beside the Thabor gardens in Rennes.

When she left with her suitcases, her father said on the doorstep: 'You're doing this to spite me.'

When she arrived in Algeria after independence, she was blinded by the beauty all around her. She had to cover her eyes with a scarf after crossing the gorge at Palestro, where wild flowers had reclaimed what had once been a battleground.

When she moved in to their small fifth-floor apartment in Algiers in 1963, the neighbour across the landing saw her with my sister in her arms and said: 'I don't wish to alarm you, Madame, I merely want to warn you. I see you have a baby. You should keep a close eye on your child. I'm a gynaecologist, you can't imagine the things I see, the damage I have to repair.'

Remembering

In Rue Saint-Charles I lose my Algerian accent. I don't want to draw attention to myself at school, among my classmates, I've already missed the beginning of term.

By the end of October, my transformation is complete. I speak 'normally', I tie my hair back, I dress in blouses and tight velour trousers, black cycling shoes with leather laces, just like all the other girls in my year. I don't answer any of the letters my friends in Algiers write to me, I'll never see them again. I tear up the photos of our last school trip to the Roman ruins in Tipasa, then I tear up the pictures of my last summer at the Club des Pins, at Moretti Beach, Algiers Beach.

I won't let myself be held back by unhappiness. I'm fourteen years old and I'm erasing my past.

Becoming

Ely's group accepts me straight away. I feel safer now that I meet up with the girls before we go out to the Kat. I've been followed twice recently, the same man both times, in a coat, with a hat. The walls of the city press down on me.

I read about men and women who become ill from repressing their homosexual needs. Suppressing your urges is dangerous. It can lead to madness or violence of some kind. Like forcing blood to flow backwards through the body.

I think about my French great-uncle who kept his lovers hidden throughout his short life, his affairs with sailors in the port city where he lived with his wife and children. I refuse to be like him. Secrets always come back to haunt you in the end.

Ely invites us to her place in the 13th Arrondissement, an apartment she's just bought with money from an inheritance. Her mother died. She drinks to forget what she calls her 'personal tragedy'. We feel at home in her flat. Some of the girls stay the night, sleeping on the couch, on the floor.

Ely has to have the lights on at night, with music playing, she's afraid of the dark, afraid of being sucked in by the blackness and never coming back.

Remembering

In Algeria, I often fantasize about disappearing: in the field of daisies that grow to my childish height and clasp at me like carnivorous plants when I plunge into their midst; at our 'spot' in the countryside where, long after it became our favourite haunt, we found a well one day, hidden beneath the long grass.

As we drive up to the ravine of the Femme Sauvage, I lean out of the window of my father's black Renault 16 so I can take the wild woman of the legend by surprise as she kneels unseen on the rocks or clings to the tree roots. One day I think I catch a glimpse of her, her long hair covering her breasts. I dream of burying my head in her bosom, of disappearing inside her.

In our apartment, my sister and I create a space from library to living room by leaving open the folding doors that divide the rooms; we spend our time there, playing ghosts.

Real life frightens us more than the supernatural.

Becoming

Ely can't cope with reality; that's why she drinks.

We're walking to the Kat along Boulevard du Montparnasse and she starts thumbing a lift. She's drunk. A police van pulls up but I refuse to get in, I carry on walking. I spend the whole night waiting for her to show up, worrying about her. Back at my flat, I'm convinced she's been raped by the police and locked up in one of their cells. She doesn't answer her phone.

The next day, she calls me, offers no apologies: 'I went to a bar with the cops, I lost track of time. You know the Tropicana? I'll have to take you there.'

Remembering

My mother is driving her blue Citroën GS one day when she's stopped by a gang of boys. They've stretched a wire across the road, she has to get out of the car. One of them beats her with a stick. As if on cue, the others all drop their trousers and taunt her with cries of 'Filthy French bitch!'

We're at Le Français, the cinema on Rue Didouche-Mourad, watching *Dance of the Vampires*. Halfway through the film we have to get up and leave. A boy has put his arm round my shoulder, grabbed me by the neck and licked my ear.

We come out of the cinema and my mother takes me to the Drugstore, a shop that's just opened in the centre of Algiers, to buy me a toy by way of consolation.

I choose a miniature skeleton.

In the El Fellah bazaar, a man puts his hand on my mother's crotch. She doesn't react. She walks over to the supermarket shelves as if nothing has happened; maybe she's ashamed, she knows I saw.

At the till, she says: 'I've learned how to ignore things for which there are no words. Without a name, nothing can exist. Do you understand?'

Becoming

It's Tuesday evening, I'm at the bar in the Kat. I see her sitting at a table close to the dance floor. There's a falling away – a falling away of space, light, music, the women around her. She draws everything in, or rather her body draws everything to her. It happens in an instant. I want her to be my first, like the opening scene in a film; her skin, her kisses will bring me good luck, she will be my talisman.

She doesn't stay. I feel bereft.

Her name is Julia. That's all I know.

Remembering

In Rue Saint-Charles, we go to the cinema with my mother three or four times a week. She says film is more powerful than real life, film takes life as its inspiration and transcends it. I have no idea what this means, I think it might be something to do with going into a trance.

The careers adviser at Keller School gives us a form to fill in. To the question, 'What do you want to be when you grow up?' I answer: 'Film director.' She glances through my file and, seeing my last name, she asks me: 'Do you speak French at home?'

Rue Saint-Charles doesn't feel to me like exile. I need to become French again, as if I'd neglected my Frenchness in Algeria; there, nature was my world, nature was where I grew up, sleeping in poppy fields, feasting on flowers. I put all my faith in treetops, in the light glancing off the Mediterranean.

France is an outfit I wear; Algeria is my skin, exposed to sun and storms.

Remembering

My mother says of Algeria, 'I'm finished with this country,' as if she were talking about the end of an affair, the fading of desire.

The wind slams the doors and windows shut, bends the eucalyptus trees in the forest of the French Embassy whose gardens we share. My mother is standing outside beneath the awning: 'I'll be blown off my feet,' she says. In my mind she's telling us what she wants to do – to take to the skies and leave us behind.

I place a bedside lamp on my desk, with a ream of paper, pencils and pens; I put on a white shirt and one of my father's ties. He lets me pick one out when he's home at the weekend, on Saturday evenings – Thursday evenings after the country adopts the Muslim calendar.

I line up the words, one after another, and I play at being a writer, a male writer. It's always a man I see.

Becoming

Ely never asks me to kiss her, she doesn't find me attractive. 'I'm not into Arabs. I know some people are crazy about them, not my thing though. I mean your skin's nice and tanned in the summer, but it's a bit sallow in the winter, know what I mean?'

Ely knows all the girls. You only have to ask her for a name, first or last, an address, and she comes up with it on the spot. When she can't actually remember something, she manages to get the information she needs from asking her 'informers' – no one can say no to her.

Her friends divide into two categories: the girls she's spent at least one night with and the ones she's had a fight with; some girls belong to both groups.

I don't have to push Ely to give me Julia's address. She warns me to be on my guard: 'She's not right for you.'

Remembering

I spy on my mother.

I sometimes think of her life as a mystery I have to solve in order to throw some light on my own life, to help me to make more sense of it.

The apartment in Algiers has several red-tiled balconies, the largest of them leading from our parents' bedroom; a row of reeds protects it from view, but my mother never sunbathes naked out there, nor even in a swimming costume. She reads her books fully dressed, out of respect.

She clutches her novels to her breast, she mustn't be disturbed. She closes her eyes, and I have the feeling she and her books go to sleep together, skin to skin, as if the books were alive.

She reads Yves Navarre, Jean-Louis Bory, Wilhelm Reich. She folds down the corners of the pages, underlines passages, breaks the spines of her books, opens them out as if they were bodies, spreading their limbs. She takes possession of them, rereads them, quotes them from memory, collects them.

They devour every inch of space in the apartment, in the library, the bedroom, sometimes the kitchen. She thinks about them all the time. She doesn't lend them, she gives them away, handling them as if they were her own skin and bone.

From time to time, her friend Andréa comes over with a bottle of wine. They smoke, Dunhill or Kool menthol depending on what's available, and listen to Joan Baez. Andréa has a secret we must never divulge: she's a Black Panther. I think it's probably illegal.

The men – my father and Andréa's husband – join them later in the evening, when the sun has gone down and the wind is coiling itself around the eucalyptus trees.

The men's voices mingle with the tones of the two revolutionaries. I'm sure there's a plot being hatched, we're in danger, I'm an American in a film.

Remembering

There is such a thing as a gay childhood. My childhood. No excuses are needed. There's no explanation. It simply is.

There is a history to homosexuality, a story with roots and a territory of its own. Being gay isn't a question of choice or preference, it simply *is*, just as blood has a type, skin has its colour, the body its dimensions, hair its texture. I see it as organic. The gay child is not lacking, she is different, outside of the norm, inside a normality of her own; not until later will she come to understand that her normality marks her out from others, condemns her to secrecy and shame.

I have a special place in my family: I am the one who must not be deflected from the path I've chosen, I am the artist, I'm entitled to wear disguises, to dress as a boy, to cast aside my frocks, to skip meals, to dive into the waves when the sea is rough, to threaten to jump off the balcony when I feel I've been wronged – mostly by my father's stern demands.

I come down with unexplained fevers a couple of times a year: fevers of a mind running amok.

At the primary school in Hydra, I overhear two playground supervisors talking about me: 'The worst of it is that the parents know and do nothing about it.'

Remembering

My father finds a painting in an antique shop, a portrait of a shepherdess on a piece of card so battered the artist's signature can't be made out. My mother has it framed, convinced she has the work of an orientalist painter in her possession.

The little shepherd girl is wearing a traditional Kabyle dress with blue and red patterns, she has bracelets on both wrists, curly hair; the look in her eyes is so sweet it can move you to tears. Eyes that draw you into the depths of her soul.

'I bought it because she looks so fragile,' my father says, 'just like you.'

Knowing

When my parents first met in Rennes, my French grandfather, who was friends with the police commissioner, asked for my father to be investigated.

A plain-clothes police officer followed my father in the morning as he left his student accommodation and in the evening when he went back home from the library or the university campus.

My grandfather wanted to know if my father was a political activist, if he was indoctrinating my mother. He found nothing, but he still went to see the dean with a request for the young man to be sent back to where he came from.

They asked my grandfather to please leave the premises or they'd call a security guard and have him forcibly removed.

Remembering

My mother: 'I didn't say anything to my parents about our wedding. We were married in the Mairie in Rennes, I was pregnant with your sister. We went to a restaurant to celebrate afterwards; I think I look sad in the photographs, it's mostly men round the table and no one's drinking wine. Some of those Algerian students changed once they went back to Algeria: they treated their wives differently, wouldn't let them leave the house. Your father was never like that, quite the opposite, I had to persuade him to spend more time with us at home – like a bird of passage.'

Becoming

Parties at Ely's place are preludes to our nights at the Kat. Her flat is where we get ready to go out; we drink to steel ourselves for the waiting, the fake merriment, the disappointment and craziness of the night, for the harsh reality of the morning, when we'll have no choice but to say 'who are we kidding, let's go home', tired and worn out from all the drinking.

We pass round a bottle of poppers, the quickest way to fry your brain cells according to Ely. There's a man who sometimes meets us at Ely's, a man in his fifties, we call him the Antique Dealer. I don't think that's what he really is, I don't ask – he looks a bit like a pimp. Night is a time for masquerades.

We arrive at the Kat and I look for Julia, the girl I've only seen once. I lie in wait for her, hour after hour, I focus on her, like a picture, a dream. She's not real anyway, she doesn't know who I am, what I want from her.

As the night goes on, Julia's image coalesces, merging with the faces of all the women at the Kat, taking something from each woman, her complexion, her colouring, the texture of her skin, creating the ideal face, the face of my fantasy.

I go home disappointed that I haven't seen her, almost resenting her.

I have her address, Ely gave it to me: 54 Rue de la Roquette. My head spins at the prospect of making my way over to the other side of the river; from a mere nothing, I'm conjuring an affair.

Remembering

Baya, the painter, is a friend of my mother's. She's tall, very skinny, with hands as fine as the paintbrushes she wields to create her women, women with zithers, birds, fish, their flower-print dresses billowing up on the wind I imagine whipping through the patio of her house in Blida, where we go to visit her once a month.

She squeezes lemons in her kitchen while we wait in the living room for her to reveal her latest paintings to us.

In my mind's eye, I see her adding a few drops of her own blood to my juice, to infect me with her talent.

Remembering

'The chamber of the winds', as my sister and I call it, in the apartment in Algiers, harbours countless secrets. Light and air filter in through latticework screens. Sheets hanging on the line smell of laundry soap and Ourdhia's perfume. Ourdhia looks after us. She coats herself with musk after bathing, squatting on her haunches in the washroom. She undoes her braid, lets her hennaed hair fall down her back. When I walk in on her and find her naked, she pinches the skin around her hips, on her belly, looks at me and laughs as she says: 'Look at these breasts of mine, nothing but scraps.'

Becoming

There's an odd couple in Ely's group: Lizz and Laurence. They live together in a tower block in the Chinese quarter, they never kiss in public, they're discreet, embarrassed by what they are, by what they represent – strength and fragility.

They watch from inside their bubble, listening in silence to the others; they get up from the table to dance to Prince's 'Kiss'.

On the dance floor, their bodies seem broken.

Laurence has a lost look. Her gaze never lingers on the girls in the Kat, nor on the male guests when we stay late at Ely's. She takes no pleasure in her own beauty, never ceases to abuse it, never grants any respite to her ravishing body.

She leans on Lizz, who steers their relationship recklessly, uncaringly – or so rumour has it. Laurence does speed, Es, coke, downers, uppers – you'd think she was a dealer from the way she talks, a dealer or a pharmacist.

Remembering

My mother and I can't help but become like a married couple in Rue Saint-Charles; I need to break away.

I go skating at Trocadéro, Montparnasse, the Main Jaune, Porte de Champerret. Moments to myself, carved out from my mother's time – apartment, breakfast, lunch, dinner, chatting in the living room, going to sleep, waking up, sharing the household tasks, the drudgery, shopping in Monoprix, outings to the movies, going for walks – stolen time, a way out of childhood.

I set myself free, take risks. I fracture my collarbone on the railing at the skating rink. Alone on the bus back to Rue Saint-Charles, I sit clutching my dislocated arm like one of those dolls you take apart and put away in the cupboard when they've served their purpose.

I'm punishing myself for deserting my mother.

Remembering

Towards the end of 1979 a rumour spreads in Algiers: there's a gang on the lookout for people celebrating Christmas, they have names, denunciations have been made. When Christmas is over people hide their trees in their car boots and dispose of them out of town, like corpses in detective films.

On the streets of Algiers there are more and more women wearing hijab – Iranians, we call them. Older women stick to the traditional white veil that flies up in the wind, revealing skin, flesh, beauty.

Ourdhia doesn't cover herself in the street, she refuses to give in; she's not afraid of the gibes, the insults.

She takes me in her arms and I burrow into her shoulder as she kisses my eyelids, '*Ya waladi, ya waladi*' (oh my child, my child). Ourdhia reassures me. She has the strength of a woman who's not afraid of men's violence.

She lives alone with her son, something that's frowned upon in her neighbourhood. She says her husband has joined the army, his unit is planting trees on the edge of the Sahel to hold back the desert. She's made this story up for her son, I know what really happened: she ran away from Sétif where they lived. He used to beat her.

Ourdhia is a believer. She says she doesn't need to hide her skin, her hair, to be a virtuous woman, that's not what religion is about, there's more to it than that – religion is kindness and forgiveness, these are the things that matter most. And morality too: no stealing or killing; lying is allowed, just a little, especially for children, so long as they apologize afterwards.

I watch unseen as she prays, kneeling on her prayer carpet, hands raised. Her fervour is palpable and I'm envious of it. She's part of a world I don't know, a world that seems kinder than mine.

I'm searching for a direction, one that's not mapped out for me. My mother talks about death, she says it's a release – after death, there's nothing.

Becoming

I come back from the Kat at night and write. I write to absolve myself of my homosexuality. I write to be loved.

I dream of being recognized, of books as bulwarks.

It will be years before I can rid myself of the fantasy that words can protect, mend what is broken, make everything better.

Remembering

Our grandparents in Rennes are dentists, they give us 'check-ups' when we go and stay with them; my grandfather looks after my 'baby teeth', my grandmother takes charge of my sister's, whose case she considers more complicated: 'Such lovely teeth, so badly treated over there.' By 'over there', she means: that uncivilized, distant place, those backward, inferior, foreign people – our country, us.

Almond trees in bloom, bouquets of mimosa, the creeks and inlets of Cherchell Beach and Bérard, the Atlas Mountains, the sea of dunes on the road to Timimoun, the dense, impenetrable, eternal beauty of 'over there'. What does my grandmother know of all this? Nothing, she knows nothing. She's lying.

We have blood tests, urine tests, our reflexes are checked, we're weighed, measured, examined, felt; they're determined to find something wrong, they must find something.

I'm paraded naked before a doctor: he checks my back to make sure my spine is erect and correctly aligned, my knees functioning as they should, my arches supple – a colt being vetted.

Becoming

Ely wants to write. She's decided on the title of her book: *Confessions of an Alcoholic Woman*. She always rings me in the early afternoon, when she's on her own; she hates silence, she needs to talk. I let her speak uninterrupted.

She misses her mother, she wishes she'd kissed her when she was dying, but she was afraid she'd wake up and kiss her back – the Devil's kiss. 'Now that I have a roof over my head, I'm drinking away my inheritance. I'll drink it down to the last drop, I'll get rid of all my fears and anxieties, once and for all.'

She isn't enrolled at the university, she doesn't work. I'm afraid her idleness will infect me. I ease my conscience when I skip my classes at Assas by telling myself: I have a novel to write, I need time to get my life in order, my new gay life (this is the label I give it, to help me accept myself, affirm who I am); I make promises to myself to move ahead, to experience *life*.

I try to work out the best way to approach Julia if I see her, I act out the scene in front of my bathroom mirror, knowing that my shyness will destroy any plan I make. I picture myself writing her a letter, I have her address after all, then I change my mind, terrified that she might reply, that someone might open my mail while I'm out, the postman, a neighbour, the concierge.

When Ely invites me to her place for tea, I say no, I don't want to get any closer to her, she scares me, her lack of self-control; I have limits she'll never be able to respect. Ely has a bad reputation and I don't want her ruining mine, even though I'm still a complete unknown, a hanger-on, a part-time member of the group – when there's one fight too many I disappear for days on end.

I don't belong to anyone.

Remembering

In the gardens of our apartment block in Algiers, there's an electricity substation hidden away at the entrance to a dirt road that leads to a platform we call 'the terrace', a square of smooth stone exposed to the sun, encircled by greenery.

Boys and girls gather there, lying on top of one another like crocodiles, soaking up the energy of the sun, the warmth of the stone.

People say there are cables running beneath the terrace that send out electrical impulses; they don't hurt but you can feel their vibrations. They fortify the blood, transform it.

I catch my sister there.

Concealed in the bushes, I watch as she is transformed before my eyes, set free from our childhood. How I envy her.

Remembering

Everything in Algeria seems strange, because of the war, because of the blood spilled on the land, in the fields, beneath the arches of the Roman ruins high on the cliffs above the sea. Violence is etched into the land, unending violence.

My mother says Algeria is an accursed land, that's why she loathes it as much as she loves it.

She's found a way to go on loving Algeria and still feel safe there: she escapes from the city. She claims the people from the south are kinder, that we have much to learn from the Tuaregs.

She organizes our trips, decides where she wants us to stay; my father phones the mayor of every *wilaya*, every district on our route. He tries to talk her out of taking the Citroën GS, he says we should fly.

We set off, my mother, my sister and I, with friends, the same ones usually: Henri, the cultural attaché at the French Centre, his Italian wife, Paola, and their son, Giovanni. Ali and his mother come too.

Ali and I have been friends since primary school, he lives in a house down the road from us. We're two of a kind, doubles almost – it upsets us that we aren't perfect doubles. We have a tendency to fuse together into one person, which worries his mother: she's afraid Ali will turn gay from associating with me.

My father oversees our preparations, and then flies off to North America and Venezuela. We don't know where he's staying nor when he'll come back – this is how my parents *work* as a couple: by retaining an element of mystery.

Remembering

'We'll never know what the ingredients of love are, how people are put together,' my mother says when I ask her what happiness means to her. 'The truth is that you can never really know another person, there are always surprises, both good and bad: reality sets in, stronger than the relationship itself, stronger than desire, the spell of being in love wears off. You have to be able to accept it: life isn't a dream, we aren't here on this earth for a life of constant pleasure; it's the difficult times that matter, much more than the lighter moments.'

Remembering

I open the mailbox and recognize my French grandmother's writing on the envelope. She always writes in the same blue ink, indigo, I see it on the cheques she sends us for the birthdays and Christmases we don't spend in France.

My mother reads the letter aloud.

My grandmother writes about her new holiday home, the spring and autumn tides, walks by the sea with her dachshund, the cliffs at La Varde, her days at work that she's finding more and more tiring; she wants to retire, her legs hurt, her knees, her wrists; staring inside other people's mouths all day is no way to live.

Sometimes she slips a hundred-franc note in the envelope, even though she knows it can't be converted to dinars.

My grandmother loves my mother in her own way, like a child one no longer understands and keeps at arm's length. She says she'll help her daughter as soon as our mother decides she's had enough of this country; my grandmother is convinced it's making her unhappy.

My grandmother has never accepted my father. She doesn't give her reasons, the real reason, she just doesn't accept him; it's a physical thing, and cultural too – 'Why couldn't you have married a boy from here?' Algiers is too far away for her liking. On the rare occasions she does come and visit she feels out of place, as a woman, a Frenchwoman. 'The poverty here is not pretty,' she says.

She fears for us, her two granddaughters, she's sure our growth is affected by the heat, by our diet.

I have difficulty drawing up a family tree, a 'tree of love' as some call it. The branches of my tree don't flower, or if they do, the blossoms appear on the wrong branches, as if they've migrated, bloomed from the soil or on a branch not meant to bear flowers.

This is how I feel about my French family, it doesn't work, it never will; it makes me uncomfortable, as if I'm outside my real self, as if I've failed to love my whole self.

I feel the same with my Algerian family. I hardly know them. They live four hundred kilometres from Algiers, you have to drive along the coast road towards Petite Kabylia, in the east. My Algerian grandmother doesn't speak French, I don't speak Arabic, our only link is her tenderness, her hands in mine, in my hair, on my shoulders, her kisses on my forehead, her smiles; but this gentleness is beyond me, I don't know what it means, I don't know if it's an expression of love or a way of apologizing for being so unlike us, for not wanting to be like us.

We are so very different.

Becoming

I go over to Julia's neighbourhood, Bastille. In the metro I look around, in search of a girl or a boy like me; I don't see any.

I'll have to get used to this new form of isolation: to being unlike other people. I don't know if I'll be able to bear having to hide, to lie, the fragility this engenders. It can drive you mad – living a double life.

I think about Laurence, harming herself because she is gay. We all do it, for the same reason; my drugs are fear, anxiety and the negative image I have of myself. I don't like myself. I'm not ashamed any more, but I don't like what I am, that hasn't changed; I wonder what I can do to start liking myself more, to trust myself, to recognize my own worth – it may not be much, but it's all I have, I'm aware of that. Will another woman give me what I'm lacking, by desiring me?

On Rue de la Roquette, I look around, searching. The women all look like her; I gaze at them one by one, my heart starts to beat faster every time, but it's never her.

The image of my mother appears, superimposed on Julia's, then melts away – I say goodbye. I feel sad, I'm afraid of bad things to come. I punish myself, again. I walk past number 54 on Rue de la Roquette without stopping. I walk all the way to Père Lachaise Cemetery.

If I am to live, I must leave my childhood behind.

Knowing

My father arrived in Marseille on a cargo ship at the end of the 1950s, took a bus to Toulouse, a train to Paris and then another train to Vannes where he spent a year at school as a boarder before he passed his *baccalauréat* – he worked hard, came top of his class despite starting at a disadvantage; he adapted, survived, but he hasn't forgotten the journey, the cold, the items in his suitcase – one suit, three white shirts – nor has he forgotten what he was told after the war was over: 'Your brother died with the guerrillas, his body hasn't been found but one of his comrades made it to Tunisia where he kept a promise he'd made to your brother. He phoned Radio Tunis and requested a song by your favourite singer, Mohamed Abdel Wahab. He asked that the song be played for you in the name of the one who loved you more than anything else in the world. May God hold you in his embrace.'

Remembering

I walk down to the Place d'Hydra with my father, my hand in his, wearing tracksuit bottoms with a white tank top and flip-flops.

I'm allowed to dress as I please. My role models are the boys of Algiers on their home-made skateboards, hitching rides behind cars and trolleybuses, my wild, crazy brothers, handsome, muscular, free, playing their reckless games. I dream of joining them.

They're the same boys who insult my mother, expose themselves to her, lust after her. I share their violence, but I turn it against myself.

My father and I do the rounds of the shopkeepers, the butcher, the grocer, the baker, the florist. They run their fingers through my short hair, they do it to greet me, to show they accept me – at least that's how I see it.

I stay glued to my father's side. I'm with the men, one of them, I'm a man, my father's son.

Remembering

We'd chosen her dress together during a visit to Paris, at the Emmanuelle Khanh outlet store on Rue Pierre-Lescot. There were no changing rooms, I held her bag, the clothes she handed to me. She went behind a clothes rack to change.

It was a yellow dress, with small red and black hearts, a low neckline. My mother looked at herself in the mirror and said: 'It's a bit like a bridesmaid's dress, I'll buy it.'

We're not allowed to talk about her being attacked, it's a closed subject, a secret room with a hidden key.

I wonder who in the town has nails long enough to rip through fabric like that.

Remembering

Ali and I are brother and sister in violence. We're a danger to other people, to each other.

He 'comes up' to my place and I 'go down' to his; we have our own geography, a geography of our bodies, a force that pulls us together and pushes us apart when the tensions between us outstrip the pleasure of getting together, being together, inventing a single person made up of the two of us, half female, half male.

We spend whole weekends together when my sister stays over at her friends' houses; I'm excluded from her circle because of our age difference. I wait with Ali for her to return, though he's not a substitute for her. I worry for her when she comes home in tears and locks herself in her room to listen to Serge Reggiani or Léo Ferré; she doesn't talk about what's making her unhappy. It's different with Ali, we tell each other when we're angry, when we've done something wrong.

We prowl through the gardens of the apartment block, two maniacs in search of fire, we invent magic potions in our bedrooms, at his house, at my house, poisonous concoctions to destroy our foes; our enemies abound, we're afraid one might overpower us, crush our deadly, invincible, unrivalled partnership.

Our energy is sexual, devoid of tenderness; our bodies are drawn together, they break apart, come back together, not in desire, but like conjoined twins taking their strength from one another, preparing to ravish an imaginary prey together.

We're children, making up stories about women, love affairs, break-ups.

Ali doesn't ask why I use the masculine form to talk about myself, he accepts it quite naturally, that's why we're friends. I'm not like other girls, I'm not really a girl. He's attracted to the boy in me, he's the one who usually ends up in tears at the end of the day.

I wipe away his tears with my right hand, the hand that was choking him a few moments earlier. I call him my 'river'.

Each of us is invaded by the other; my sister captures Ali's voice one day on her tape recorder, and his is the voice I miss the most when our box of cassettes disappears.

Ali is the first to see me for what I really am – a flesh-eating plant.

Knowing

My mother was born before the Second World War; she lived through the bombing raids, and this gives me another reason to admire her.

I picture the sky black with planes, but my mother says it wasn't like that: 'We couldn't see the planes at first, we heard them getting closer and then all of a sudden they erupted and rained bombs down on the city.'

As soon as the siren sounded they had to go down to the shelter. It was her favourite moment, like a game. There she was, underground, with the neighbours from Rue d'Antrain, her parents, her brother, her two sisters, it was like being in a cabin. It was magical to think this could be their last night, exhilarating to be confronted with the fragile nature of things and relationships.

The war marked the end of her childhood.

As the bombs fell close to their building, shaking the walls of the cellar they were sheltering in, she felt an overwhelming love for her family, more powerful than any she had ever felt before.

Her father was different in those days. He was gentler, more caring. It was a time of heroism. One night, he had a prophetic dream: their house, destroyed in an explosion.

They moved to a farm in the country; their house in Rue d'Antrain was bombed soon after they moved. The farm was paradise, the animals my mother looked after were so much more docile than people. She'd never known happiness like this before, wouldn't experience it again until she travelled in the desert in Algeria, going back and forth from one village to another, camping out at night, life in the wild.

Her father decided the family should stay on the farm until the end of the war. He owned the farm and his land was rented out to local farmers; he'd built an empire 'by the sweat of his brow', as he liked to say – it was his favourite expression.

He carried on working and came home to visit his family once a week, by car or on his motorbike. He owned five dental offices in the area, including one 'mobile' office that went everywhere with him. Nothing stopped him; all he wanted to do was 'tend' patients and 'amass wealth', or so my mother would say whenever she was angry at this father who worked too much and loved her too little.

In the countryside, rationing tokens and hardships were a thing of the past.

My mother pictured the city reduced to ashes.

Her new life was better, by far.

Remembering

In my new incarnation, I wander through the shopping centre at Beaugrenelle. I think of it as a ship. I run around in the square in front, beneath the concrete tower blocks.

I'm searching for my lost childhood. I've started my life again from scratch, without the incomparable light of Algiers that once illuminated my days. I'm losing my way.

I have no trouble fitting in at school, despite being so different. I've tried to stifle my otherness but it goes deeper than I realized. My vibrations must be out of tune with the other girls' but luckily no one seems to be turned off. People seek my company, I'm the perfect companion for skipping school, breaking the rules; I make everything seem like a game, I'm tough enough for two, I come from Algeria, that feared land of dreams. I have an advantage over the others, I know about life – I've hardly lived yet but I've seen both the light and the dark sides of life.

I spend as much time with boys as I do with girls. We watch a film at one of the boys' houses one day, *The Story of O*. We stop the tape at the parts we find most tantalizing – scenes of abuse and submission.

I don't tell anyone, but I've read the book the film is based on; much of it was lost on me, but I understood what it said about power and its pleasures, about the satisfactions of dominating and being dominated.

The book was in my mother's library in Algiers. I read it sitting on the carpet in the living room, the sun's rays slicing into my back, the words like daggers on the page. I wasn't shocked, I recognized the violence in those words; they opened avenues of desire in me I hadn't known existed, showed me that pain could lead to ecstasy and gave me an image that will always be with me, of two women together.

Remembering

We mark out our route to the south on the map.

It will take us across the small desert, through El Oued, El Goléa, through the great desert of the trans-Saharan route, past the oil wells of In Salah, then towards Adrar, Tamanrasset, the landscape unfolding before us, a succession of vistas: sand, earth, rock. I picture the Sahara as it appears in prehistoric cave drawings, with strange beasts, lakes, greenery. I imagine the force of the earthquakes and volcanic eruptions, the terror they must have awakened; this is where we began, in this cauldron, this chaos, I know it, I feel it. I feel it when I'm drawing in my bedroom, sketching the portrait of the faceless man, the alien; I feel it again later when I see the same image on a rock in Tassili and wonder if I'd really seen it when I drew it or if I'd invented it, in thrall to the phantoms of the desert.

My mother wears leather gloves to drive, her palms too sweaty to grip the wheel. We peel oranges for her, she needs the liquid, it's all we can do; it calms her nerves too though she tries not to show how scared she is. 'Sing me that song "Breakfast in America",' she says whenever she has to overtake a petrol tanker. The road is narrow, like the valley of death – if my mother's steering is off by just a few centimetres we'll be smashed to pieces.

Becoming

Elula, the owner of the Kat, asks us to leave. A woman has smashed a glass over Ely's head and Elula's afraid it'll turn into a brawl. She's been trying to keep a low profile in the neighbourhood since a crime was reported on Rue du Vieux Colombier.

The mafia control the nightclubs. The police provide protection for the Kat. I have fantasies of secret deals – protection in exchange for girls and a share of the takings. I make up all kinds of things. I'm waiting for Julia.

I don't want to leave. I try to dissociate myself from Ely. She's just forced herself on a girl in a couple, kissed her. I thought it was funny, but love between women is no joke, it's life or death from the word go, there's more at stake here than the simple fact of being in love: finding love means being saved. I understand, although Ely says that real love never lasts more than two years, especially a love born of the night.

Elula eventually grabs hold of my arm: 'You too, get out!' People assume I'm part of Ely's group, even though I'm not really.

I was hoping to see Julia, I was waiting for her as I do every evening at the Kat, and now I'm out in the street with Ely, Lizz and Laurence. We head for the Seine, in search of a bar; it's late and the cafes are all shut except the ones on the Grands Boulevards so we decide to walk over there.

Ely, standing on the wall of a bridge, threatens to jump off. No one takes her seriously – Ely loves life too much, girls, drinking, partying. I sometimes think she's invented the story about her mother, that things didn't happen as she claims, she didn't inherit that much money, she says it because it makes her feel secure with the girls; she'd like to be able to buy them, to buy their love. Money is her safeguard against loneliness. She's got it all wrong though, she knows she has, she drinks to forget she knows. Ely's young but she's afraid she'll end up by herself.

We keep walking towards the other side of the river, ignoring her insults: 'Wait, you bitches! Wait for me!' I keep my distance. Laurence walks over to me, Lizz tries to shove her away, but Laurence says: 'It starts slowly, you know, it has to work its way into the brain, little glimmers at first, kind of like a light bulb, that's it, little filaments lighting up inside my head, one at a time, inside my body. You have to be patient, it comes on gradually, especially if it's just smack, a smidgen, that's all I ever take. I've got it all under control. Lizz doesn't believe me, but she doesn't know how good I am at it, or else she doesn't want to know – she has a low opinion of me, thinks I'm stupid, talks down to me, doesn't tell me anything important. We hardly talk to each other any more, not since we moved in together, you know. I thought it would bring us together if she moved in with me, but it hasn't, not in the least, not even in bed. When we're together, it's like she's drawn an invisible line between us, a line I'm not allowed to cross, no wonder I'm off my head after that. She stays because I'm beautiful. I'm not bragging, I know how good I look, not that I'm proud of it, it's got nothing to do with me – sometimes I'd like to be shot of it, I'd like people to like me for myself, for who I am inside, not for my eyes, my mouth, my body, no, but for all the thoughts I have that make up who I am, for my past too. Lizz doesn't know a thing about my past, she never asks, she doesn't want to know. She doesn't want anyone else to have me either, she'd be jealous. I'm just one of her possessions, something she's added to her collection without really noticing, something she doesn't want to give away, and all the time I'm crazy about her, even though she's cruel to me, or maybe, now that I think about it, maybe because she's so cruel to me. We're all a bit masochistic, aren't we, let's face it, it's not easy loving women. It's a big mountain to climb, you never get to the top, it's always shrouded in mist and there's no light up there, and all this stuff, coke, uppers, Es, it's to break up the fog. You don't get it, any of you, but I have to live with it every day. I can't see the light unless I'm wasted, that's when I see the truth, and when I look into your eyes, I can tell you're a good person, you're not cut out for this whole scene – it'll drag you down, you wait.'

Knowing

After the Liberation my grandfather found a new house to buy in Rennes, near the Thabor gardens; the house in Rue d'Antrain had been completely destroyed, reduced to a crater. My mother says that being a survivor gave her a different perspective on life, with the possibility of death woven through it – fate alone can decide and it answers to no one.

The new house was spacious, with six floors, an attic, a garden, a kitchen garden, one large living room and one smaller salon, the blue salon, decorated in the style of Madame Lanvin's boudoir, complete with tapestries, velvet sofas and armchairs, china, medals and collectibles; my grandmother didn't know that her last days would be spent in this room, that she would die there.

My mother says it all started with this house – the depression, the violence, the fear – she believes a house has an effect on its occupants. The walls are its memory.

When they moved in, they found German army uniforms in the kitchen, with champagne glasses, a birthday cake – the party had been interrupted.

Her father became stricter, he was like a madman sometimes, no one ever knew why. He would lock her in the basement with her brother when they misbehaved. Her mother was distant, cut off from the family, treating them either with pity or with indifference; her work was her refuge, work that gave her no pleasure.

From time to time, guests would stay in the bedrooms on

the upper floors; the house was more than big enough, there was plenty of room. My grandmother loved to entertain, she came back to life in the company of other people: the clairvoyant who conducted seances with her, the artist who painted portraits of her three daughters, Monsieur B., a childhood friend of my grandfather's, who my mother describes as if she were evoking a character in a film, a film whose images live on, images of a life that isn't real, a life gone by, erased by the passing of the years.

Remembering

In Algiers I see shadows moving across my bedroom walls at night, coming towards me and retreating, entities with a life of their own. I'm sure they're trying to communicate. I keep myself awake, praying they'll reappear. I lie in wait, hoping for a sign.

I put more faith in heaven than in life on earth. Because of Ali. He wants to kill me, I know it. I'm part of him, his darker side – I have to be eliminated.

We're with his mother in Zeralda, a beach resort about ten kilometres from Algiers. The water is grey and cool, not good for swimming. Jellyfish lie washed up on the sand by the dozen. We poke at them with a stick to empty them of their transparent liquid – we think of it as their blood.

There's a strong smell of seaweed, it's nauseating, it smells of death, or at least as I imagine death would smell, over-powering, intolerable.

Ali's mother pays no attention to us, she's reading, she looks up to gaze out at the horizon, she seems so sad – behind her sunglasses she's crying.

She's French, like my mother, but she doesn't like Algeria or Algerians, she wishes she could leave, walk away from it all, she confides in my mother every day, at the school gate, at home or on the phone. My mother says sadness that doesn't go away can be a real illness, she says you can feel it under the skin, coursing through the body like a virus, moving from head to heart, from heart to stomach. Ali's mother is sick with sadness, it distorts every word she utters; we shouldn't believe anything she says, none of it is true, the illness is eating away at her, detaching her from other people – without a cure she'd be just as unhappy in France or in America.

Ali and I escape the beach. We leave her to her solitude.

We climb the boundary wall of the Hotel Zeralda, bougainvillea tearing at our bare skin. There's a pool in the gardens, its water royal blue, like the sky in May. Colours stand out, each one clearly defined, it's dazzling; we're besotted with one another. This area is out of bounds, reserved for guests of the hotel; there's no one here, not even a lifeguard, just Ali and me.

He gives me an odd look: 'How about a diving competition?'

He climbs up on the diving board, dives in, I go in after him. We dive in again, taking turns, ten times or more, we keep going. It reminds me of the film I saw on television a few days ago, *They Shoot Horses, Don't They?*, it was just like this, the same atmosphere – you can't give in, whatever happens. Ali knows I'll never give in, it's the way I am, fanatical; he's physically stronger than I am, but mentally, I'm unbeatable. I have something to prove – I'm a girl.

Then the dive that's too much: too much energy, too much sun, too much blue sky, too much red, green, yellow blossom. My head hits the water. I black out, sink to the bottom, my body is rock, sand, sun, whirlpools; no longer mine.

I resurface, try to swim, but I've forgotten how, I go under again. I sink to the bottom of the pool. I'm hypnotized by the little blue squares, I think I'm in a blue room, my French grandmother's salon, a room in a museum, in the Louvre, in a king's bedchamber, a queen's; it feels good, I want to stay. I've left my body, I'm suffocating, I have to do something.

I push myself up from the bottom and sink down again. Six times. Every time I come up I have a fleeting glimpse of the sky, so inconceivable, so sad, inconceivable because it is so pure, sad because this is the last time I'll see it: I'm dying, I'm watching myself die.

I manage to call out to Ali, I utter the words for the first time, words that stick in my throat; half crazed, I shout, 'Help! Help!', but there's no response, I sink back down again; I'm all alone, there's no one to help me.

I come back to the surface one last time. Ali is standing on the side of the pool, arms folded. He looks me in the eye and backs away towards the bougainvillea-covered wall that separates the pool from the beach – he's leaving me.

I sink. I sit cross-legged on the bottom for a few moments, my hair floating around my shoulders like the jellyfish we saw on the beach.

I think of my mother, how despairing she'd be if she were to lose me. I don't want to drive her to her death. Eight is no age to die.

I say to myself: 'Not yet.'

A column of light forms on the surface, sucking me upwards. I come up fast, without realizing what's happening. I don't believe in God, I haven't been taught to believe, but I know I've just been saved by an invisible hand.

I climb over the wall, exhausted. I walk across the beach, trembling from head to foot, my arms and shoulders shaking. Ali, sitting on his beach towel, looks at me, that strange look again. I say nothing, sit down next to him. His mother asks me: 'Where were you? Look, here's your tea: bread and butter with chocolate spread, would you like that?'

Becoming

There's a woman at the Kat I can't stop looking at, in a white burnouse with a red chechia, a hat like a fez. She's tall, you notice her immediately in the crowd because of her clothes, her manner: she's elegant, mysterious, other-worldly – sometimes there's a mist around her, or a gleaming halo, depending on the way I look at her. She never stays for long, perhaps there's someone waiting for her outside. She prowls round the club, like an animal patrolling its hunting ground, looks about her, chooses a woman, or not if no one takes her fancy, then leaves: the night is hers too.

Back home, I write about her. She keeps me company. In my imagination, we spend the night together.

I write to love and be loved, on the page. I live out my dreams as I write – I have affair after affair, fictional liaisons in which I conquer my fear of women, of the unknown.

Remembering

I love my sister, I don't want anyone to take her place, but I yearn for another sibling, a third child in the family, a boy who will stand in for me, free me of the role I'm expected to play. I didn't choose to play this role.

I am seen as the missing son, by everyone.

One day I realize this brother will never appear. My mother has to go to hospital. My parents' sheets are stained with blood, my mother is 'bleeding from the vagina'.

I imagine a two-headed monster inside her, trying to break out, wounding her.

Remembering

We discover a rock jutting out into the sea, eighty kilometres from Algiers, a secret place just beyond the village of Bérard that I think of as being like the womb. To reach it you have to go through a farm, down a steeply sloping road, into the bowels of the earth, red rocks, trees crowding together and blocking out the sun, a magical forest like nowhere else in the world. The giant rock forms a peninsula – flat, perfectly smooth, polished by wind and salt, a platform for us to launch ourselves from, like birds taking flight. Legend has it that the currents here are criss-crossed with the fresh waters of a river, waters that once restored a princess's sight and now bestow happiness on lovers.

Becoming

Ely calls me in the middle of the night. She's been drinking, I can hear it in her voice. She's come home early to talk to me, she has something she can't wait to tell me: she's seen Julia, told her about me, shown her a Polaroid she'd taken at her place that she keeps in her wallet – it's always a good idea to keep a photo of a nice-looking girl on you. She uses me as her alibi, I know she does, I don't mind. Ely has a soft heart – it's impossible to hold anything against her.

She says: 'She's sold on you, I did a great job of talking you up, you wouldn't believe it.'

Julia is currently unattached, which terrifies me: I'm on a list, the next girl in line, I'll take my turn and be replaced afterwards by another girl.

Ely's set something up for me, on a Tuesday, at the Kat: 'Julia'll ask you to slow-dance with her.'

I can't sleep after I put the phone down, I wrap my sheets around me, gripped by a mixture of fear and the urge to finally live out my imaginings. The unseen, my fantasies, will become flesh.

I feel so small, a tiny speck in my bed, in this city, this country, this continent. I've cast off my bindings, I no longer have a name, I'm ageless, homeless, with no past, no family; all I have is a future, a future that will plunge me into another life.

When I think of Julia, I remember her as being rather coarse.

Knowing

My mother arrived in Algeria just as the French, the colonizers, were leaving. She felt she had a mission, she saw herself as a representative of the French people, the French people of France and the French people of Algeria, bound together by ties of love and friendship. She brought a message of peace. She came with proof, evidence for those who refused to believe: her children, the fruit of that love.

She learned enough Arabic to get by, passed her driving test, swore that we would know our country from the inside, not as French children but as Algerians, which resulted in my French grandmother saying to me during the school holidays: 'I can see you're not one of us, always walking around with bare feet, little savage.'

I picture the ships pulling out of the port with their cargo of tears and regrets, setting out to cross the Mediterranean, venturing over the waves, towards the horizon, towards a new life in Nice, Marseille, Toulon.

The *pieds-noirs* stayed in the south, across the sea from the land of their birth. The French no longer considered them French. Nor were they Algerian. With no nation to call their own, they saw themselves as spiritual orphans, alone in a country they didn't know, marooned in a foreign land.

In years to come, children of mixed marriages, children like me, would be referred to as second-generation *pieds-noirs* – history repeating itself.

Remembering

Throughout the 1990s I am consumed by Algeria's anguish. I mark the location of every massacre on a map, places where I felt the sun's warm kiss, where I swam to my heart's content in the sea, at one with nature and her laws, the Mediterranean my kingdom where I braved the waves undaunted by the dangers of rip tides and undertows. I knew no fear.

I become obsessed by one particular scenario, I see it played out before me in images as if projected on my bedroom walls. I ought to write it down to free myself of the obsession, but I don't. I call it 'Project Zero' because it seems to me that all my subsequent writing stems from this one tale. I can only remember fragments.

'At nightfall, they cut off the electricity to the villages they plan to besiege, the village is plunged into darkness, the inhabitants taken by surprise, unable to flee, unable to defend themselves . . . lookouts armed with guns guard the entrance to the village, the attackers use knives, axes to massacre the villagers, they rip open the bellies of pregnant women, tear out the foetuses, throw them from balconies, rooftops, place them in other women's bellies . . . they behead people, reattach their heads on others' bodies, cut off hands and fingers to take rings, bracelets . . . infants are found in ovens, scraps of flesh pinned to fencing, to roof tiles, spattered on the ground where explosives have been used . . . one man said blood was falling from the sky, he thought it was raining blood until he saw the corpses impaled on the branches of trees . . . another man said: "I know who they are, these people, they'll come back, they'll slit the throats of survivors." '

Remembering

The Grenel is open on Sunday afternoons. I'm fourteen, there's no entrance fee, it's dark inside, small rooms tucked away, benches and red stools, furniture typical of the early eighties; I'll see it again in provincial clubs and in the *Milieu des filles*, the lesbian scene, as if my days of carefree existence began and ended then.

I like parties, or the prospect of a party. It's not so much joy I feel as the thrill of being in a place that's forbidden (the Grenel isn't but it feels that way to me), of living a secret life (a forerunner of nights at the Kat), of always doing things behind my mother's back, not as a way of betraying her trust, but to grow up, breathing in the smoke and alcohol fumes around me, although I don't actually drink, I'm too young.

I gaze admiringly at the girls and boys chatting together, kissing, swaying sinuously on the dance floor, their bodies supple, electric, dressed in jumpsuits, shorts, white T-shirts; it's hot, summer's coming. I feel free and I glory in my freedom.

Remembering

1993. A pharmacist we know is found in her house, her throat cut.

She's lying on her sofa, her face resting on a cushion, a pack of sleeping pills and a bottle of spirits on the coffee table. The police say something isn't right, there's nothing to suggest it was an act of terrorism, nor a robbery gone wrong – the door hasn't been forced, there's no sign of a struggle, she wasn't taken by surprise in her living room. She must have spoken to her attackers, offered them a drink perhaps, and then just like that, with no warning, her throat was slit, in one swift movement. The wound is clean, like a line drawn on paper with a red pen, there's virtually no blood on her chest. It looks like a settling of accounts, but there's nothing in her past, she was well liked in the neighbourhood. She'd been separated for several years from her unfaithful husband, she'd chosen not to remarry, she was a very attractive woman who 'lived like a Westerner', although her sister says she never flaunted herself, she was careful, especially recently, wary of the bearded men that came into the pharmacy and knew who she was.

The investigation stumbles until her son Tarek goes to the police and admits that he asked three of his friends to teach his mother a lesson; she didn't live as an honest woman should. He hadn't ever seen another man in the house since his father left, but even so, he couldn't bear the shame any longer.

He's convinced she was using her charms somewhere else,

behind his back, exploiting her beauty, which he says burned everything in its path.

I knew Tarek.
We'd been on a trip to the desert together a few years earlier, with Ali.

Knowing

Monsieur B. came to stay with my grandparents a few months after the Liberation. He hadn't recovered from the war. He'd spent a year in a concentration camp and he was ill, he'd contracted typhus, lost weight, he was traumatized and couldn't be left on his own, he had to have people around him, needed reassurance. My grandparents went to fetch him from his house in Angers; they came back to Rennes with a man who was like a wounded animal. They had to look after him, be gentle with him. My grandmother said there were no words for what he'd been through, he needed his friends, his closest friends, they were like family to him, and the children brought him so much joy, they gave him back his will to live. They feared for him, he was so thin, so weakened, unrecognizable, it was so sad to see him in this state.

My grandmother promised him he'd get his strength back in the house by the Thabor gardens, she would take care of him, not as a patient, but as a survivor admired for his courage, and as soon as he was recovered they'd take him to the coast, where the sea would wash away his sorrows.

Monsieur B. stayed for six months, longer perhaps, my mother doesn't remember, she doesn't want to; he slept in the yellow room, close to the children's room.

At first, they fed him sugar water, with a teaspoon, and then he gradually regained his appetite and with it his strength, his bulk, his muscles. He was still too afraid to go out in the street, but he would walk in the garden, burying his face in the roses, gathering the raspberries that grew along the fence. He'd sit in the sun when the weather was nice on a wrought-iron chair, reading the paper, not books – he couldn't concentrate for more than a few minutes, his mind would start wandering and he'd think about his future, what he'd do once he was back in Angers, his home. He wanted to open another patisserie, he had the money and he'd never been afraid of hard work. He wasn't easily cowed – after what he'd been through he could endure anything. He felt free, he was happy; life in the house in Thabor had showed him the way back to that well of happiness he thought had run dry.

In the morning, he'd get up very early, he loved the quality of the early morning light; he'd have his coffee in the drawing room where the light came in through the French windows that opened on to the garden, then he came back upstairs, without a sound, like a cat, something he'd learned during the war: how to dissolve into his surroundings. He would become each stair, each square of earth, each corner of the building, he was wood and stone, glass and steel, velvet and cotton, he was sound and silence, birdsong and dogs barking, he was invisible and omnipresent, dream and reality, inside and outside, he was and he was not, truth and illusion, eternally secret, he was the sheets, the skin, the hair and the eyes of the little girls he came to visit every morning because children were what he loved more than anything else in the world, slipping into their bed to embrace them as they had never been embraced before.

Becoming

The woman who runs the cloakroom, opens the doors and vets the clients is called Mariem. She's African. She's been working for the club since it first opened. Elula took her under her wing, like a gang leader looking out for a weaker member.

Mariem wants to look like Tina Turner, she copies the hairstyle, wears the leather skirts and tight dresses. I don't know if she likes women. I don't know anything about her lovers, she hoots with laughter when one of the girls comes on to her. She has one passion, her son – all her hard work is for him.

Mariem says the night is a whore, it brings with it both darkness and light, hope and disappointment. She tries to protect herself, advises me to do the same, especially with me being so young – there are other places to go and have fun, other people to meet, in the real world, outside in the pavement cafes, in the sunshine; after midnight it's all fake, everyone's wearing a mask, hiding.

My face is an open book. Mariem calls me 'Baby'.

When I have no one to walk home with, no one to give me a lift, I wait with Mariem until first light. I've stopped going home by myself in the dark.

I'm often the last to leave the Kat. No one pays any attention to me, I don't bother anyone. I watch people, I'm deep inside the lesbian scene, I'm part of it, assimilated, accepted. A new family, so different from my own: Maryse wiping down the bar, Elula and Aymée adding up the till. Sometimes one of the waitresses opens a bottle of champagne; they don't offer me a glass, I'm the child who shouldn't be there, but people like me so they let me stay.

Outside in the dawn light, I feel protected by the sun as it rises.

We go our separate ways after Rennes metro station, home to bed ready to come back together for another evening. It reminds me of a Ferris wheel going round, my head starts to spin; even when there's nothing going on, anything could still happen. Time stretches, I'm living out of sync with other people, with night and day.

Death no longer exists.

Remembering

There's a Chinese clinic in Cheraga, on the outskirts of Algiers. They practise a different kind of medicine there, preventative medicine, according to the brochure that's come through the post.

My mother has asthma, she goes for treatment once a week, on Wednesday afternoons, when I don't have school; she chose to have her appointments then so I can go with her.

At the clinic I wait in the corridor. Seeing the nurses makes me feel ill too, the doctors in their white coats with masks over their faces.

I'm bored waiting for my mother. I go down to the basement. Four foetuses float in jars on a shelf. Swollen eyelids, eyes wide open. They stare at me with a look that says I've walked in on their conversation.

The smell of formalin goes to my head, I feel woozy, run back up into the room where my mother is, where she's told me not to go.

I open the door and see her there, needles stuck all over her face, her hand in the hand of the doctor treating her.

Becoming

I'm wearing black – trousers and a thin roll-neck top.

I've lost weight. My homosexuality has obscured my childhood, my adolescence, my younger self. New ideas, going out at night, obsessions, repressed desires have made my body anew.

The day of my meeting with Julia has arrived.

I write a few pages, rip them up, afraid they might be discovered if I don't come home. My fantasies of disappearing return.

The thought of meeting her is linked in my mind to a kidnapping, the first kiss to a crime. I'm the only witness to the revolution I'm living through, I have no one to confide in, no one to tell of my fears, my excitement; my family would never understand and Ely laughs at me at the slightest excuse.

Ely asks me to come to her place before I go to the Kat. She'll come with me, of course. I say thank you, although I'm not sure I really want her company.

She's useful to me, like a flashlight in the dark, and she uses me too. We've come to a sort of tacit understanding. I act as her alibi, her confidante, she knows I'll listen to her complaining, her stories – I'm never shocked. She trusts me, knows I don't gossip. I keep it all to myself, not out of consideration for her, but out of self-interest – her stories will be useful to me one day for my writing. I'm not ashamed of thinking like this, of being short on scruples.

Ely is waiting for me. She's wearing a suit, she looks older.

She opened a bottle of vodka earlier this afternoon but I refuse to drink with her. 'You're no fun at all.' She's right. I'm no fun, because I'm scared. Night seeps into my veins, polluting my blood. I start thinking about AIDS.

I know nothing about Julia; no one knows anything about anyone else.

I want to ask Ely if she's been tested but I don't have the courage. She's out on her balcony, smoking, gazing up at the sky. She throws me a barb, irritated: 'I'm only doing this for you, I mean, I don't even like Julia, and Tuesdays at the Kat are a nightmare.'

I already love Julia. I love her the way I love every woman on earth tonight.

I'm propelled by desire, on the crest of a wave. Ely can't stop me, she knows it, I think she's jealous.

'We're nothing,' Ely says in the taxi, 'nothing at all, just dust, nothing but dust'; the driver looks at me in the mirror and I feel like telling him this is my big night, I'm taking the plunge.

We drive past the Jardin du Luxembourg. I see Julia's form in every tree.

We arrive at the Kat to the sound of Stephan Eicher singing 'Combien de temps', the perfect soundtrack for what I'm about to go through, although I don't realize that yet.

Ely says hi to the girls she knows. I feel like running away but I stand firm. I focus my thoughts on the island near Bérard, my sister's friends, their skin glowing in the sun. It was there, on that rock suspended between sea and land, that I understood the bliss of being alive.

I sit at Ely's table, near the bar, waiting for a signal; nothing happens, the club is almost empty. I keep hearing the song going through my head, over and over again, 'Combien de temps', how long, Ely's words echoing in the background: 'She'll ask you to dance when they get to the slow numbers.'

I ask Ely if she's seen Julia: no, she hasn't, maybe she isn't coming, it wouldn't be such a bad thing, it'd teach me a lesson, I should learn to be more flexible.

I feel a hand take me by the arm, urging me to stand. I offer no resistance. Julia's a pro when it comes to slow dancing, the art of seduction, she knows what she's doing, she's sure of herself, and so she should be, she's stunning, even though there's definitely something trashy about her. She's beautiful – it's the way she is, the way she moves, the way she carries herself.

She's wearing a white blouse tucked into black ski pants with heels and an ankle-length coat. She presses her stomach against mine, runs her hand through my hair. I'm shaking, I hate myself for it. I'm a novice; eighteen, still a child. I think about young men who go with prostitutes.

I can feel Julia's body against mine; it's my first time dancing with a woman. It doesn't seem weird, there's nothing indecent about it, but still, it's odd.

The song comes to an end and she cups her hands around my face and kisses me. I think of the women of Algiers in the stairwells of our apartment block, who used to seize me by the neck, 'Boussa, boussa' (kiss, kiss), I think of the eternal mother figure, locking her child in a brutal embrace, so intense is her love for her child.

Julia invites me to her table. She introduces me to Sophie, her best friend, and to Gil, who I mistake for a man. Gil shakes my hand and says: 'Isn't it past your bedtime?'

Sophie is tall and blonde, an airline stewardess for Lufthansa, she wanted to be a model; she's not tall enough for the catwalk but she sometimes does lingerie photo shoots.

Gil has short curly hair, fine features, a boyish frame. She owns a clothes shop. Gil and Sophie met three years ago at Bains Douches. Sophie used to go with men. She says it's no different with Gil, just better. She's not interested in girly women, she's not even sure if she really likes women. It's not the same with Gil, it's something completely different, she doesn't quite know what to call it.

I feel like leaving the Kat, Paris, getting on a plane and going back to my family, thousands of kilometres away in the Gulf. I feel alone, cast adrift from everything that's 'normal' for me.

Julia wants to see me again the following Saturday, at her place. She gives me her number, I don't give her mine. They leave, offer to drop me off, I say no. I don't want them knowing where I live.

I can't find Ely. I stay behind at the Kat. I watch the women on the dance floor. This place exists in a time zone of its own, inside and outside of time. We're a realm apart. We always will be. Lesbians.

I watch a couple dressed in three-piece suits, like the Gigolas of Pigalle in the 1930s. One of them walks with a cane, her piercing blue eyes shining like lasers in the darkness.

I walk home later, I've shed my fear. I walk quickly, fleeing from what I've just been doing, dancing cheek to cheek, skin to skin, the kiss.

I'm at one with the sky, the wind, the clouds scudding across the moon. Paris moves through me, carrying me, helping me: I'm ashamed, ashamed of who I am.

Remembering

In the Atlas Mountains the landscape transforms, expands.

Sand works its way into the engine of our car, our blue Citroën GS that rises when it starts up like an amphibious vehicle preparing to cross a river; my job is to make sure there's a coating of grease on the bonnet to keep the sand out.

The Sahara is a land of its own, we marvel at its softness after the violence of the city. We are afraid of nothing here, not even of losing our way, we're watched over by the village people who welcome us with milk and warm bread.

We keep a medicine chest in the boot and my mother puts me in charge of handing out eyedrops, aspirin tablets, plasters, mercurochrome; my sister is responsible for distributing colour pencils and biros.

The children who throw their arms round me are my age and yet I feel older than they are, older than the other members of this new family that sets my heart racing.

The desert changes me. Our travels teach me to see things that are invisible to others.

Knowing

When the war came to an end, my mother wanted to go and see the house she'd lived in before it was bombed.

There was nothing left to see. The garden had absorbed it all, her bedroom, her toys; a part of her would remain forever out of reach, a chapter of her life story buried beneath the earth that closed over it after the bomb fell.

Her childhood had been symbolically ruined, she would never again be able to inhabit it, take pleasure in it; she learned early on how destructive men can be.

It was about that time that my grandfather took her to a bullfight in the arena in Nîmes, to teach her about life, about resistance, about what it means to stand and fight; he thought of her as a boy, stronger than her brother, whose health was fragile.

He was disappointed to see her crying at the sight of the blood gushing from the bull, from the flanks of the injured horses. She begged to leave the arena. Out in the street, the city burning in the summer sun, he called her a pathetic weakling and said: 'No good will come of you, my girl. You mark my words.'

Remembering

A man comes to see my father in the middle of the night. He doesn't ring the doorbell, he knocks, waking me up.

He's my father's foster brother. He's 'an important man' according to those who know him. He used to be in the resistance, he's biding his time, waiting to go into politics. My father admires him, thinks he can do no wrong. There's no warning of his visits until the very last minute. He feels under threat, he's convinced they want to 'get rid of him'.

My father takes him into the kitchen so they can talk in peace. I hide in the hall, watch their shadows moving beyond the glass door; my mother makes coffee, sets the table, serves up the leftover lamb or fish.

The man makes no eye contact with her, he treats women as inferiors, my mother complains sometimes to my father, who responds by saying: 'He's a leader.'

He and my father both participate in the negotiations to free the American hostages in Iran at the end of the 1970s. You can see the foster brother in the press photos, in the foreground, signing the accords with a member of the US government. My father is standing behind him, holding a cigarette, gazing into the lens through his tinted glasses, his face partly hidden.

This photograph sums up my father – he's there but he's not really present, a prince with his crown in his hands, trying to keep it out of sight.

Becoming

I call Julia the next day, despite Ely's advice to wait a few days before calling her: you should never show weakness with a seasoned player like Julia, she'll crush you pitilessly if you do.

I'd be happy to be crushed by Julia. I'm not afraid of being hurt, being alone is the only thing I find truly sad.

Julia suggests we meet on Saturday. I make a note of the entry code and the floor she lives on. She's an old hand at this, she's not afraid of inviting a stranger to her place, I'm the one who's scared, and suddenly I feel a surge of terror – I've given her my number.

I spend my days waiting to see her in a parallel time zone, beyond the city, outside my own body. I don't go to the university, I don't write, everything is an effort, fear takes hold of me, fear of not being able to go through with it.

I phone my mother one evening, she's just come back from the beach. 'You sound funny, is there something you're not telling me?' My mother thinks I'm having trouble at university, that I'm finding it hard to fit in.

She's right, I do have problems. How am I going to do this? What exactly is another woman's body, a woman other than myself?

I don't go to the Kat on Friday. Ely disapproves of me saving myself for Julia – 'You're already at her beck and call' – and then starts telling me about how she's so worried about Laurence, who she says is acting more and more weirdly.

She's either doped up on sleeping pills or high on speed, Lizz can't take any more of it.

Laurence is moving away from us, heading for dark waters, beyond our reach.

Ely asks me to speak to her, I'm the new one in the group; I can't, I say, I know nothing about addiction.

Laurence says drugs are her haven, a kennel she retreats to like a dog; she says we should leave her alone.

Remembering

My mother has a need to escape, to be outside herself; she has blackouts.

She calls the cabin staff during a flight back to Algiers after a week in Paris and then passes out.

They lie her down across three seats at the back of the plane, use a sheet as a makeshift screen, remove her make-up; one of the stewards brings an oxygen can and a mask from the cockpit.

I understand my mother. She wants to be taken care of, she wants to put herself in the hands of experts who know what to do, she wants them to cure her, comfort her. She's right, we're not up to the task, we don't know how to heal her wounds, her unhappiness. Calling on experts is the right thing to do.

I hope I'll be saved one day. I hope I'll find the women who will come to my rescue.

I feel ashamed as passengers turn and look at us, wanting to know if it's serious, if the young blonde woman with two little girls is going to die or not.

I stare out of the windows at the clouds, bouquets of pink and white, I look down on the fields, set out in straight lines, like the squares on a chess board, yellow, green and brown, the landscape of Algeria.

Remembering

Ali lays two bolsters across his bed, lowers the wooden blind in his bedroom; warm air comes in through the open window, folds itself around our feverish bodies. We're playing brothels; we each have to select an imaginary woman, lie on top of her and pleasure ourselves; then we fire up his Scalextric and bet money on the winning car, usually his. He cheats, I know he does. I let him do it, my mind is elsewhere, troubled by the secret game we've made up; we've promised ourselves we'll never tell anyone about it, never play it with anyone else – we are brother and sister now, together in pleasure.

Knowing

My grandmother used to hold seances and commune with spirits, she read minds, had prophetic dreams, sensed vibrations and knew the good from the bad, she could make the hands on her watch move, and on the clock in the house in Thabor. It was a gift, she said, an uncommon gift of magnetism. She went to church on Sundays, was wary of bad luck and evil spirits.

My mother told her one day what Monsieur B. was doing, not accusingly, she made light of it, dropping it into the conversation, saying it didn't affect her, she was merely trying to protect her little sisters. My grandmother told her there was a word to describe girls like her: 'spiteful'.

Monsieur B. continued to come and visit, on his own at first, and soon after with his wife, for as he said to my grandfather, a man shouldn't stay single for too long, it's not good for the blood, for the spleen.

He'd met her in Angers, they were getting ready to open a third patisserie together. He really loved her, as much as it's possible for a man to love a woman; men and women are so different, fundamentally incompatible, but that was another matter entirely and he had no desire to discuss it.

When he couldn't accept my grandparents' invitations, for Christmas, New Year, Easter, summer holidays, he'd send them some of his renowned chocolate truffles by post.

Remembering

Roadblocks spring up all over Algeria during the 1990s, fake road closures. People are murdered in the woods, on mountain roads in Kabylia, by the beaches; no one knows where to expect the roadblocks, how to avoid them.

People stop driving at night, in the half-light of morning, they pray they won't encounter the assassins sowing terror amid splendour – beneath the cliffs, atop citadels, in the streams and valleys that rise from the mist, in sunlight and darkness, masked men, in disguise, armed with knives and axes.

I picture the birds, squirrels, wild boar, stray dogs witnessing these scenes. I wonder if they're aware of the horror, the suffering.

The backdrop remains unchanged, the landscape of my walks and discoveries, where I gained a sense of belonging to a world that is vaster, richer than my own: of being part of the earth, the earth that carries within it all the promises of the future, my future.

Everything turns to blood, grime, mud, fire. An apocalypse. They are murdering my childhood.

Knowing

She couldn't hold my gaze. My eyes were strange, enormous, almost bulging, disquieting; she felt she was being judged.

I looked like an alien to her. I was different from the babies she heard wailing in the neighbouring rooms. I was quiet, I seemed to be saying: 'So this is life then, and this is the way you are, my mother.'

I was funny-looking, I wasn't as attractive as my sister, who was born with a full head of hair, a perfect little doll; you couldn't tell what I was, I could just as easily have been a boy.

It was very hot, the last day in July. She'd been admitted to hospital the evening before and I was born at half past midnight. It was a painless birth, as it was for my sister, thanks to the Russian professor's methods. Then I was 'wrenched away' from her and put into an incubator for a few days; I was too small, three weeks premature, I needed to be cosseted in a plexiglass womb.

She was afraid of not getting me back, of not recognizing me. I'd vanished.

When I came back, something miraculous happened: I stopped being an alien, I became the child she'd been expecting.

The flame of love can be slow to ignite, she says.

Becoming

Julia is wearing a military shirt, I can see her lacy bra, her skin; her dark hair flows down her back, over her shoulders. Standing there in the doorway of her apartment, barefoot, she seems even more ravishing than at the Kat.

She lives in a top-floor studio. It's quiet, no noise from the street, from Bastille, the bars, the people, the traffic chaos. In the courtyard, two trees that have grown together. I've stepped outside the city, outside myself, outside everything I've ever been or ever will be, everything I know.

I go inside, glance at her bed. I say to myself, accusing, applauding: 'I'm gay.'

I'm leaving my childhood behind.

I think of my grandmother, who used to say of me: 'You'd have to pay that one to go out with a boy. She's a brainbox, or else she's a lesbian.' I'm proving her right and it galls me. How could I have known that accepting one's nature would prove so difficult?

I take off my coat. I daren't move closer to Julia, I'm afraid she'll kiss me, press me to her, pull me towards the bed. I'm scared, and I want her. It would have been much simpler with a boy. I'm face to face with two realities, two sources of strength, two points of weakness: my nature and my virginity.

Fear must be written on my face. Julia holds back. She seems so much more adult than I am, and yet she's barely thirty years old – I promise myself I won't think about my mother.

Remembering

It's the summer I turn fourteen. We're in the mountains, near Chambéry, in a meadow. In spite of the splendour of the peaks, the glaciers, I'm suffocating here, hemmed in by two mountain ranges, as if trapped by life. My obsession with death has taken hold – one day all this will come to an end. I can't accept it. I think it might be to do with sex, I read that somewhere. Sexual frustration.

I imagine infinity as a spiral that will carry me away.

It's a physical phobia, it gives me vertigo. And yet I'm in the grip of something greater than myself, more powerful, better too, and with this simple thought I start to feel better.

I'm borne along by beauty, poetry, the sublime order of nature, this is my religion: the wind in the trees, the colour of the leaves as they turn, waves foaming on the shore, the sun slipping away and rising on another continent, the stars, the rivers and springs, the earth moving, its fiery core that I sense beneath my bare feet, the flowers that taste of fruit when I chew them – I draw strength from all this, my elixir of eternal life.

Nature protects me, bears me up towards the light; I put my trust in her, I lower my eyes and salute her.

That day, my mother has a revelation. I hear her talking to herself: 'If I don't do something soon, we'll never leave.'

She folds the blanket we're sitting on, packs up the water, the fruit, the slices of strawberry shortcake, puts them all back in the ice chest, picks up the magazines she's left open – my mother buys all the papers, she finds it comforting. We go back into the village, she has to make an urgent phone call. I don't ask questions, I follow along.

I hear her talking to my father on the phone, it sounds like a lovers' tiff, they have them all the time. They blow up like storms and melt away as quickly as they came.

They love each other, despite their differences. It comforts me to think this. They are my castle walls.

That night, I can't sleep, unsettled by this sudden change of plans. The next day we take the train to Paris. My mother leaves me there; she's going back to Algeria without me, she says I have to wait for her in Rennes at my grandparents' house, with my sister, who's at university there.

August draws to a close. September arrives. I miss the start of term at the lycée in Algiers.

I feel as if I've been ejected, thrown by the wayside. I kill time in the Thabor gardens with my little cousin Camille in her buggy, and her mother, Franka, my favourite aunt, who looks like Jenna de Rosnay, and my sister, who I think is in love.

Every detail matters. Details drown out my sadness. My sister is wearing a white V-neck T-shirt, slouchy jeans and a yellow army belt.

A few weeks later, I'm in the garden in the late afternoon when the phone rings. I hear my grandmother's voice: 'I see, I see. You need to tell her. I'll pass her to you.'

My mother is in Algiers, she's organizing the move. She's planning to leave everything behind, leaving my room exactly as it is, I'm not a child any more. We'll buy new clothes, anything I want, at Galeries Lafayette.

She's found an apartment in Paris, in the 15th Arrondissement. I already know the neighbourhood, we spent a few months there ten years ago, I won't feel too homesick there.

She has paperwork to do to get me into a school, it's late September and there's only one lycée still accepting pupils, it's not the best one.

She'll call me back to let me know when I can go to our new apartment. She hopes everything will be ready for me, the furniture should have arrived – the flat isn't very big but it's bright.

We're going to share a room, she's sorry, it's the best she could find within her budget. My father will come later, she doesn't know when, but he's promised he will.

She can't stay in Algiers, she's ill; this country is making her ill. It's giving her nightmares. She knows it's going to turn into a bloodbath. She's sure it is.

I come back in from the garden, Billy Joel playing on the radio, 'Honesty'. I feel like crying, but the tears don't come. I look up at the sky and think of the Roman ruins in Chenoua, of the snapshot of me standing on a promontory facing the sea, my body swaying in the wind.

Becoming

I scan Julia's bookshelves, her bits and pieces, her Carlos Jobim albums, novels by South American authors I don't know.

Julia is Colombian, she left her country because of the cartels; I act like I believe her. She's studying photography in Paris but she keeps running into difficulties, her life is a series of tests, hurdles to overcome. She misses her family but she feels safe here.

Her photos are of nudes, encircled by ropes, plastic, chains, the faces obscured, the skin taut, muscles flexed, veins bulging. The human body fascinates her, especially dancers' bodies.

She asks me what I do for a living and I say: 'My parents think I'm a student, but I'm writing – I know, I'm only eighteen, but it's what I live for, writing and love.'

She picks up a rosary lying on a table, kisses it: 'Your time will come, you'll see, you'll blossom, like the flowers in the field when the time is right.'

I don't know whether she's talking about writing or love, her words make sense either way; I'm putty in her hands.

Remembering

In Timimoun, I feel free. We've driven a long way, past the oil wells that scorch the skies of In Salah, past the turning for the road to Adrar, through landscapes of rock and scrubland.

The tall, red gates of the city rise before us, Sudanese architecture, palm groves – life exerts its power here, water flows in abundance, cool and fresh, giving life to trees, flowers, crops. The soil here produces miracles. We're staying in the hotel built by Fernand Pouillon in the days of the French. Nothing bad can happen here.

I believe in a world beyond this one, a world of legends and djinns. A Tuareg asks me to place my left hand in the sand so he can read my future in the handprint. He smiles as he sees my anxious look. It's not the prospect of finding out what the future holds that worries me. I'm afraid he'll see who I really am.

Remembering

In Algiers, my father receives a phone call from an 'official': his foster brother's small private plane has crashed in a forest near Bamako. A search is under way, access in this location is difficult.

He gathers us together to tell us how worried he is, how despairing.

He thinks I have supernatural powers and asks me to concentrate my mind on his brother being found safe and sound, opens the atlas to show me where Bamako is in Africa.

The news comes through one morning. He's alive, but battered and broken, according to the official who's been giving my father daily updates. The pilot and the rest of the crew didn't make it. It's a miracle he survived. I like the sound of the words 'miraculous survivor', I make them my own.

A few months later, he talks to my father about the crash, the noise, the silence that came after; he was more concerned about poachers and animals in the forest than about what had happened, all he remembers of the accident is the dull thud of the impact, a streak of light across the cockpit.

He was thrown from the plane, he couldn't move. He survived by chewing on roots to extract the liquid from them while he waited for help.

I imagine a jungle inhabited by dinosaurs and giant plants, like the ones in the adventure stories I read. He's a hero.

I learn a new expression, 'terrorist attack'. He vows revenge.

Becoming

I don't let Julia know that this is the first time I've kissed a woman.

She presses her stomach to mine. I can feel her sex and I push her away. I don't want to feel it.

She says: 'If you don't even try, it's not going to work between us.' I picture a system, of nuts and bolts, wires, mechanical, clockwork; I don't know, I don't want this.

During the night, Julia brings herself to orgasm in three minutes.

I close my eyes. I see the fields of blue thistles along the road to Koléa.

I fall asleep in her arms, listening not to her heart but to the heartbeat of the woman I imagined she was before I met her, before I heard her as she climaxed, thinking not of me but of another woman.

Remembering

I'm four years old when we leave Algiers for the first time, in 1971. My father has been posted to Paris, with a bank affiliated to the one in Algiers he's been working for since he finished university.

He accepted the job in Paris for my mother's sake, for ours too; he feared for our future as mixed-race girls in Algeria.

It's autumn when we arrive. We move into an apartment on Rue Gutenberg in the 15th Arrondissement. I remember a thick white carpet I liked to play on because it was warm from the underfloor heating. The red-brick walls come back to me, the bare trees, the smell of the boulangerie, of croissants, the metro, random images: my father in his beige overcoat, the phone ringing, a grey metal lift, my mother and her sheepskin coat, her perfume, Chanel No. 5, my sister and her 'memory book' – her friends had all written in it for her, or left a photo or a collage – my Happy Families cards, Shetland wool sweaters, rubber boots, the empty space in the new apartment we never manage to fill because it's only temporary.

We don't realize it, but we're just passing through.

Leaving Algeria was a tragic mistake – we miss the light, the gardens, the trees, the perfume of the blossoms, the smell of rain on the earth, living free in nature.

Here, we are bowed down by the rain.

Rue Gutenberg lasts for two or three months. Then it's the train, my grandfather, a compartment with red bench seats, the sound of the door sliding open when the conductor comes to check our tickets, the landscape through the window, names of towns – Le Mans, Laval, Vitré, Rennes – the house near the Thabor gardens, the bedroom my sister and I are given, with a chandelier, wooden floors that creak with every step, a fireplace, a cherub on the mantel, a mirror, an antique wooden writing desk, my sister's canopy bed that we turn into a cabin, a tent, a bunker, my smaller bed. They don't want to separate us but we each have our own bed, on the same floor as our grandparents, close by if anything happens.

My mother is there. I don't know how long for.

She settles us in, reassures us, tells us this is only temporary, we mustn't worry, the house is new, with a garden, a dog, a cat, I'll have a lovely time, no need to cry, I'm a big girl, a brave girl, I'm four years old, she'll be back in no time, she promises; she and my father have business to attend to.

It's all a blur, I can't unlock my memory, I don't know the code. Hard as I try, I can't find it. The combinations are infinite and something is blocking me, something greater than I am; there's a rope tied round my ankles, I can't move ahead. Perhaps I don't want to, the prospect fills me with dread – I've forgotten in order to remain in ignorance. Rue Gutenberg, was it before or after Rennes? Did the apartment exist or have I dreamed it up?

Every evening we wait for our mother to call. She says she's in Paris; I can hear the emptiness in her voice. I want to talk to my father. She says he's busy, he'll call back. He doesn't call.

My sister and I make arrangements to combat what she calls our 'sense of displacement', big words for a nine-year-old.

She says we've been uprooted and I imagine a tree trunk ripped from the earth, with us inside the tree.

At night, I climb into bed with her. I'm scared of the dark, I miss my mother, even with the scarf doused in her perfume she gave me to help me get through the week. She comes back at the weekend, though sometimes she's away for longer, I don't remember, the weeks and months are a blur. I'm with my sister, I'm sure of that, her skin against mine at night, my mother substitute, my double; later, with women I meet, women who love me, women I love, I try hard not to slip back into the sad and tender cocoon of those days.

Becoming

When I sleep at Julia's, Ely goes to the Kat with the rest of the gang.

She says she's depressed, she misses me. I don't believe her, Ely doesn't need other people to have a good time, she just wants someone to listen to her, someone to make her feel alive, but it's all one way, she doesn't make other people feel alive. When she looks at you she zeroes in on the slightest defect in your outfit, your attitude, she can make you feel humiliated without saying a word. It's a knack she has, quick-fire judgement, instantaneous, she's never wrong, which is why it hurts.

Ely's uncompromising nature is partly to blame for Laurence's unhappiness. They were together for a while, not that long, but long enough for Ely to break Laurence's heart by cheating on her right in front of her one night when she was 'messed up'.

Ely reckons alcoholics shouldn't mix with junkies, the two don't work together, they're on different journeys with different ways of thinking. Alcohol welds you to the ground, drugs send you hurtling skywards. Ely likes to feel the ground beneath her feet, beneath her hands when she falls. She's wary of clouds, mist, fog. The sky is a passageway to death.

Ely tells me what happened to her the other night.

There was an actress at the Kat, a woman who'd been in a film with Jane Birkin. They'd done a sex scene together, although Ely doesn't think either of them is 'that way inclined'.

Ely's never wrong about women's inclinations. She can tell when a straight woman is on the verge of changing tack, she can sense when a woman is denying her own sexuality. She can tell if someone is receptive or closed off. Some women can't be deflected from men and however hard that may be for us to understand, we have to respect it. Ely is of the opinion that men and women weren't made to be together, they're too different. She doesn't go along with the idea of complementarity. When you're with someone that different, you end up losing your essence, your sense of self, you waste all your energy trying to be more like the other person, but it's futile, a battle you'll never win.

With another woman, there's no threat of being overpowered, we're evenly matched and it stays that way; we're equals physically, and even if one of us is stronger mentally, there's none of that business of one person taking control.

Ely says it's important to remember that certain men are the enemy: it's part of their violent nature. She advises me to be on my guard with men, you never know what their lust will turn to if it's thwarted or scorned, and it's pretty clear that I have no use for male desire.

I tell her she's wrong, I'm not like that, at least I don't think I am. I'm just scared of men at night.

Ely says it'll be years before we can be proud of who we are, other people won't let us, but the day will come when things will change.

The Actress had two girlfriends with her as well as her producer and her agent, a tall man who Ely said doubled as a bodyguard.

He kept his eye on the girls clustered around the Actress, watching their every move, as if they were planning to grab hold of her at any moment, touch her, spike her drink, it was ridiculous. There was a buzz in the air, the girls on the wrong side of the dance floor, the *losers*, were asking for her autograph, Elula was getting jumpy, but things were still under control.

And then Laurence lost it. She'd taken speed. Lizz had left the Kat earlier, claiming she was tired, but Ely thinks she had a date with another woman, or maybe with a man – she'd walked in on her in the bathroom reapplying her make-up, fixing her hair and spraying herself with perfume before she left. Ely felt bad for Laurence, it's always the same, every time.

No one can fix what's wrong with Laurence, no one can contain her, she's an unstoppable force.

Laurence wanted to talk to the Actress. They told her it wasn't possible. Ely was staying out of it, but she was watching it all closely. Laurence was convinced she'd met the Actress in another life, she said they had a connection, this was a sign, she had to seize this chance, she couldn't let it slip, it's bad luck to miss an opportunity like that.

There was no point in telling her it wasn't true, that she had to stop, the agent could get violent. Laurence kept insisting she wanted to talk to the Actress, just a few words, it was very important, she had a message to give her.

Then she accidentally knocked over the glasses on the table, she put her hand on the Actress's thigh, and after that it all happened really fast, like in a film. The agent smashed a bottle and threatened her with a piece of broken glass: 'You touch her again and I'll cut you open.'

Ely said it was as if Laurence wasn't there, as if the drug had devoured her flesh, her bones, as if she were just an empty shell, as if she'd left the land of the living.

Remembering

My mother has gone to America with Andréa. They went in a small aeroplane, to make it easier to fly to out-of-the-way places. Andréa was planning to visit some Mexican friends, but that's all my mother could tell us, it's confidential, and we're too young to understand.

They were caught in a storm while they were flying over the Bermuda Triangle. Everyone knows the islands emit magnetic waves that confuse navigation instruments, and the plane went into a dive. The pilot managed to stabilize it but my mother says they almost skimmed the water. Cognac was served to the passengers, which is always a bad sign, but my mother wasn't scared, quite the opposite, she realized she was experiencing a moment of rare intensity, a moment to be treasured in spite of the danger – we need danger to show us how attached to life we are. She learned more about herself in those few seconds than she had in many years: she's stronger than she realized, and even though she loves us, her daughters, more than anything else in the world, she has no attachments, she accepts whatever fate has in store for her, and if she'd had to die during that flight, so be it, that was what was written and there's nothing anyone could have done; and better still, she felt a kind of relief, a pleasure almost, in staring her own death in the face, in being the heroine of her own life, being fully present in the experience she was having.

My mother tells us this story with a Barry White record

playing in the background, a record she'd heard in the TWA 747 taking her back to Paris before she came home to Algiers.

All songs are linked to my mother in my head, her mysteries, her contradictions – sadness and joy, shadows and sensuality.

Remembering

In Rennes I go to the Thabor nursery and my sister starts her first year at the Duchesse Anne Primary School.

My grandmother works part-time so she can pick us up in the afternoon. She becomes a mother again, but this time she's patient, loving even. A kiss from me can melt the stoniest of hearts, even my grandmother's.

She gives in to all our whims: ducks, rabbits, a tombstone for a dead blackbird, sleeping with the dachshund, his velvet ears smelling of hazelnuts, making crêpes, playing shop, getting out the scales and the till, dancing, singing, jumping in piles of fallen leaves, in the snow, picking the first roses, going to look at the sea.

I cry less often. I'm beginning to feel at home in this big house that harbours a secret in every room. My mother's voice on the phone is growing stronger, the emptiness has gone, she'll come and fetch us soon; I want to stay here, I've grown used to my new home, my new friends, I like Sundays at my great-grandmother's, she cooks for us – chicken casserole, potatoes, roast pork, stewed fruit, chocolate mousse – she buys us cakes at the boulangerie for our tea in front of the television, watching Gérard Majax's magic show. I want to be a magician, transform reality when it doesn't suit me, tell stories the way I like them, with happy endings.

We play on the swings at the Parc de Maurepas near my great-grandmother's apartment, a museum filled with treasures from her husband's sea voyages: jewels, figurines, medals, pirates' loot plundered for a second time by this ship's captain bent on seducing and holding the woman who captivated men with her heady perfumes, her red lips, her possum-fur coat, her legs as long as a French cancan dancer's.

We stand tall on the swings, my sister and I, two birds in flight, unfettered, free.

Remembering

Mirages rise up before us on the desert roads: waves roll towards us, ready to break and engulf us in foam, only to vanish in a play of light and shade as we draw closer.

The mirage we see is no illusion. This is where real life is, in the depths of the Ténéré desert, as if we'd lived until this moment in a world of shadows, an unreal world that exists alongside us, alongside the truth. Not a soul crosses our path. Not a sound breaks the silence.

We are at peace, my mother says, as if she were speaking of departed souls.

Knowing

During the war, my grandparents' neighbours were arrested one morning by the French police and taken away to a secret location.

My mother was watching the scene from her window, it happened just before she left with her family for the safety of the countryside.

The neighbours were calm and resigned, obeying the orders of the officers who came to take them and their two children away; they left without any luggage, they had just enough time to grab a coat, a scarf – it was cold – then the doors slammed shut and she heard the sound of a car, of tyres screeching as if the car were making a getaway, out of control all of a sudden.

During the night, someone had daubed in black paint across the metal shutters of their shop: JEWS.

When my mother asked her mother what that meant and what they could do to help their neighbours, my grandmother replied: 'Nothing, it's best not to get involved.'

A few years later, when my mother asked her about a branch of the family we never saw, the Aschpiels, my grandmother gave a similar reply: 'I don't want to talk about it, we could find ourselves in another war some day, you never know.'

Remembering

My mother says it's impossible to say where you come from without getting something wrong. Searching for your origins is like following a winding path that branches off into more winding paths, even a family tree won't reveal the truth: families bury their secrets, it's the one thing they all have in common, they keep them hidden and if any of those secrets do come to light, they deny them.

Families are forbidden chambers of forbidden memories, sealed units that leave a trail of destruction; when I ask my mother what kind of destruction, she answers without thinking and says, just as her mother does: 'I can't tell you.'

People's lives appear to me as an unending series of unanswered questions, a web of doubts, shadows, fears and imaginings; I play out the story of our relatives the Aschpiels in my head: Central Europe, travelling, hiding, camps perhaps. Everything is hidden, kept in silence, held in check not by shame but by fear.

Families are fertile territory for fear, and I'm scared. I know nothing about my past, my ancestors; I carry their sorrows, their misdeeds perhaps, within me, and because I search where others do not look, because I see in my mother what others have not seen, I will pass those sorrows and misdeeds on to others; I will write, I will piece together the story with my words, I will create scenes that are invented, reported, true, untrue, I will bring the tale to life and stop it from haunting me.

When my mother came home with her dress torn, I was struck by the peculiar noise made by the central furnace concealed in the bushes of the gardens. In the months that followed, that sound reminded me again and again of the image of my mother half naked, her skin streaked with dirt; every time the image appeared, I wove together the elements of the story my mother refused to divulge – nothing else had happened, she said, there was nothing more to say, and so my imagination constructed another narrative, different from hers, a narrative to wrap hers in, to heal it, to smother it with light, colour, perfume, and clothe the truth in beauty.

Remembering

Village people in Kabylia take up arms against the assailants. Women and men, defending their families, their homes, their crops. They kill to live, to be free. Amid the splendour of the mountains, they wage war on fear; they spread terror and chaos while nature, the harsh mistress who has never protected them, is handmaiden to the new soldiers of misfortune. The villagers stay awake all night, taking turns to keep watch, rifles at the ready, lighting up the valley with their torches, tracking their enemy as they track wolves, to protect their herds, their chickens, their children. Their war is won in silence, in isolation; their faces covered with scarves, they film themselves so as never to forget what they call 'the second revolution'.

Becoming

Julia calls me constantly, she says she worries if I don't answer. I'm convinced she calls just before she goes out; she never answers the phone at night, I hang up as soon as her answerphone clicks on.

I learn all about lying on the lesbian scene. I'm not sure if it's to do with it being night, or if it's to do with being gay, as if all the hiding, concealing who we are to protect ourselves from other people, has made dissembling part of our nature. Words become misshapen, like well-worn clothing, over-used objects. We all lie – I lie too, about how I spend my time, what I think, what I feel.

When Ely asks me if the sex was good with Julia, I tell her to watch *In the Realm of the Senses*, that'll give her a pretty good idea. When she asks me if I'm in love, I say you can't be in love at eighteen, it's impossible, love is for old people, and anyway, there's no such thing as love, we all know that.

Ely congratulates herself, she says I've changed, I'm not so romantic, I'm more of a realist, my eyes have been opened; she feels reassured I won't be hurt. Julia can't be relied on, she's not loyal, her word means nothing, I shouldn't trust her, seriously – speaking of which, Ely was surprised to see her at the Kat during the week, without me.

I reply that I wasn't well that evening.

I'm not sure Ely believes me, but I am sure that Julia lies to me. I've known her for two weeks now, and yet I don't know her. I'm madly in love with her: she's my first and she's slipping away from me, she's hurting me.

I don't want to be hurt. I don't like being in pain. I don't want to suffer, but suffering awakens me. It opens my heart. It makes my hands shake. It makes me write – I bring the night and its women home with me, I embellish it, dress it up like a doll, write about it in the journal I call 'My Doll Bella'. I write, hoping someone will pick up my journal and read it, hoping I will no longer have to explain myself – that my writing will speak for me and set me free.

Remembering

At home in Algeria, my mother wears loose clothing, Kabyle dresses with flower patterns, djellabas, African boubous, clothes so loose I can slip inside them and take hold of her as if I am once again a part of her; we are fused together, skin on skin, flesh on flesh, two hearts beating side by side, blood on blood, life quickened by life, unbroken, eternal; my mother, a lioness, bestowing the kisses she was denied, uncounted, unrestrained, returning hugs, making wild promises, until death do us part, together forever, bonded, wedded. It's too much sometimes – my grandmother says, 'You shouldn't slobber all over your children like that'; my sister, 'You're disgusting.' We play a game we've made up, 'nose in the eye', we have a private code for when we're out walking hand in hand: one squeeze *I love you*, two squeezes *Walk faster someone's following us*, three squeezes *I'm so happy*, no squeeze at all *So nice to just while away the time together*; I dive off the rocks to impress her, climb the highest peaks, reach for the sky to fill her with beauty and poetry. I want to heal her wounds, soothe her anguish, avenge her of her enemies; I promise to cherish and protect her for the rest of my life – I'll betray her, of course – and I sing 'La maladie d'amour' for her because it's about us.

Remembering

Ali has a dog, a White Shepherd he's named Poly after the white horse that appears in his favourite books and cartoons. He found him on the coastal road, abandoned in the reeds. He fed him from a baby's bottle at first and then he cut off the end of a mineral water bottle and used that. Poly eats fruit, cereal, rice. Some say he has magical powers. His eyes are so light people think he's blind. He walks on three legs, sometimes on four, it depends on the time of year. He never runs or plays, he lies on his back to soak up the sun, sleeps outside on the terrace or in the shade. He doesn't mind the wind or the rain, spins round in circles when there's a storm coming.

The only person Poly heeds is Ali, his master.

When I come to the villa, Ali ties him to a tree with a chain. Ali says Poly is in love with me. Left to his own devices, Poly knocks me over and lies on top of me, his abdomen pressed to mine. Ali waits a few minutes before coming to set me free.

'You can't complain about being loved,' he says, when I finally stop crying.

Becoming

The women's clubs close one after another, Baby Doll, Cloud, the New Monocle. Julia won't take me to Chez Moune – she says I'm too young.

The Garage is closing down soon too, for financial reasons. It's only open for a few more nights, we have to make the most of it. It's better than the Kat, bigger. Julia is supposed to meet Sophie and Gil there, and a group of male friends she wants me to meet. I feel reassured – she's not ashamed of me; maybe's she's more attached to me than I realize.

I make my way there on my own – Julia has a dinner beforehand. I'm not invited, I don't ask who she's with, I'd rather not know.

I can see I'm not important to her. I make up stories about her, I'm floundering in the dark. I stop going to class, I don't show up for my exams, I skip supervisions; I can't take going to law school any more, I hate Assas and everything it stands for. My life is the opposite of the other students', but I can't find a kindred spirit in my new life either, the women I spend time with are my rivals, women I go out with, not my friends.

Julia is not the love of my life: there's no such thing as love.

My ID is checked at the door, and I'm allowed in. I'm swallowed up in a throng of women, a swarm. That smell of skin, hair, sweat, perfume, sex. I keep thinking of my mother, my family, the way they might judge me. I refuse to sully my experiences, and yet I feel sullied: I could do so much better.

Everything here revolves around Julia, the Black song that's playing – 'Wonderful Life' – the flashing strobe lights, the drunk women dancing, and me, making my way towards a woman who doesn't turn to look at me.

At her table are women, girls, and a boy about my age, slender, dark, with shoulder-length hair; he looks like a dancer. Our eyes meet, he smiles at me. Julia catches sight of me, stands up, puts her arm around my waist; I feel alive. I couldn't live without women, without their gentleness, their violence. Women are my kingdom, my prison.

I've given Julia no pleasure, but I belong to her. She never thinks of me, but I think of her all the time. She doesn't love me, but I'm in love with her.

She introduces me to her friends: Fred, a West Indian woman dressed as a man, short, slicked-back hair, and Martine, her wife, as she calls her, even though they're no longer a couple.

Martine is petite, blonde, dressed in a skirt with a flowery top. Fred drinks champagne, smokes cigarillos, she's wearing a print silk scarf. I count the number of motifs on her scarf while she talks to me, to distract my attention from Julia who's walking over to the boy, Sami, and his sister Nour, an immaculate brunette, strikingly pretty in spite of the scar running down the right side of her face.

Gil's not happy, Sophie's leaving her; she can't take the tension between them any more, although it used to be part of the attraction. Julia says not to get involved, they always end up patching things up and turning against the person they'd confided in. I let Gil carry on talking, I don't say anything: 'I know you think I'm the one with the problem, Sophie's always complaining about me, all over Paris, but it's not true, any of it. Honest to God, she won't leave me alone, she's always going for me, it makes me furious. It's passion, she says, that's the way it is, she likes being roughed up a bit, she gets bored otherwise, but I'm not going down that route, no way, it's not my thing. You don't hit women, ever, they're like glass. My mum, she's my goddess, you know. We're Sephardic – respect, that's what it's all about with us women. I'm not saying it's not the same for other people, but it's all to do with our mothers, you know, with women it's always about my mother, the respect I have for her, so I'll never lay a finger on Sophie, never. She's always begging me, and I've said yes just to hang on to her, but I've had enough, that's not what love's all about. I blame that guy she was with before, he damaged her, she's getting over it now but still, I don't want to fall into that trap. I've got her under my skin, though, my life's nothing without her – it's like all the water's been drained from the river, you know, there's nothing left but mud and rocks. Sophie, she's everything that's beautiful in this life, without her it's all ugly, and I'm nothing, I'm just a pawn in all this. I feel empty and I'm sick of it, she's destroying me – that's what it is, I'm being destroyed by a love that's sick, like a piece of fruit, you know, a fruit that looks delicious but on the inside, it's rotten.'

I'll be like Gil before too long: an empty shell, lost.

Nour has her arm round Julia, she smiles at me; I let myself drift with the Simple Minds track that's playing. I used to love it when I was fifteen, only three years ago – it seems like an eternity now. I've learned more about myself in the last few months than in all the other years of my existence put together.

As we leave the Garage, Nour says to Julia: 'I'll call you.'

In the taxi on the way back, I think about what I need to do to open up to her more. She's asked me to give more but I feel like I'm already giving so much. I know nothing about sex, I don't know what level of sexual intensity there has to be if you want to keep hold of the other person, if you want her to love you.

Back at Julia's, she stands at the window and smokes a cigarette. She's thinking about Nour: she'll see her again soon. She thinks about me: she's made a mistake.

Remembering

I spy on my sister and her friends sunbathing in a secluded spot. They take off their bikini tops, roll the bottoms down so the sun will reach as much of their body as possible. The wind blows the smell of their suntan lotion towards me. I stay hidden behind the rocks at the creek where we spend our days diving off the rocks, swimming, drunk on happiness and freedom, in our secret Algeria that no foreigner ever sees, in the belly of North Africa, the centre of my world, my paradise that I will never accept having lost. I left both my innocence and my virtue there.

Remembering

Ourdhia sings me to sleep with an Idir song, 'A Vava Inouva'. She's sitting on my bed, my head in her lap. Her dress is belted at the waist, her bare feet stained orange from henna; she wears fine gold bracelets on her wrists, a ring like a signet ring on her little finger – she kisses it and says that God is my protector, nothing can happen to me, I can let sleep take me, like a friend leading me into an enchanted forest.

I believe her, my eyes close. I try to resist, I want to stay with her. She is all the women and all the stars that light up my dreams.

Knowing

He arrived early, in a hurry, it was going to snow; he wasn't afraid, wasn't ashamed, he wanted to get it over with, clear the air. He'd asked to meet her, he needed to talk to her.

She invited him in, showed him to the blue salon. She closed the double doors behind them, sat on the edge of the blue velvet couch, crossed her legs, stared at him, waited for him to explain himself.

He struck her as polite, good-looking; he was probably hiding something, 'those people' always were. She was wary of them, never knew how they were going to react. She was surprised at how well educated he was, the way he expressed himself. He quoted Ronsard. He loved the French language. She had to admit he spoke it very well, better than some of her own children.

He was serious, hard-working, always top of his class. He had his faults, like everyone else, but all he wanted was for her daughter to be happy.

She listened, used words like 'village' and 'natives' to talk about where he came from.

In her world, cross-cultural relationships were unheard of.

She looked at his hands, observed his gestures, the way he carried himself, this body that slept beside her daughter's in the student lodgings where they lived. They were living on a student grant. She'd made the decision not to support her daughter – she wanted her to face up to the choices she'd made.

But she had sent her half a chicken one day when she'd heard she wasn't eating enough.

He was angry at himself for making excuses.

He spoke to her of the journey he'd made, from one country to another, one world to another. He missed his family. His brother had left to join the struggle. He hadn't heard from him since. He was very worried.

He told her he was resilient, spoke of his capacity for endurance. He'd always stood firm, he was fearless, it was his way of life, his destiny – he knew he was meant for great things. He would conquer the world, from Jijel to Rennes, from Algeria to France. He planned to expand his horizons, he gave her his promise.

He asked for her daughter's hand.

She didn't give her consent, thought it was too soon – they were too young to be engaged, they hardly knew each other, love often brings disappointments.

But he had no choice, given the situation.

What situation?

'We're expecting a baby.'

'I won't see you out. You know the way.'

Outside in the street, he felt himself plunged into darkness.

Becoming

Ely left the Kat in the middle of the night. Everything was bothering her – I was at the Garage that night. She walked towards the Île Saint-Louis and when she came to the angled bridge, she clambered up, looked down at the river and, believe it or not, she saw five faces floating in the water, smiling at her, calling her; it was terrifying, hard to resist. She came back down, looked at the faces in the water, thought about it, lit a cigarette. She had a choice, to answer their call or to carry on walking. She hesitated for a moment. It was raining, she was shivering, voices floated up from the river, louder and louder, saying her name, her real name, 'Elisabeth, Elisabeth, Elisabeth' – it made her think of a story she was told as a child, about a washer of the dead who steals a dead woman's ring, and that night, after the burial, the dead woman appears to her and says: 'Give me back my ring, give me back my ring.' The voices kept on calling to Ely. She climbed back up and jumped in. I know, it's crazy, and the worst thing is that in the Seine, with all those faces around her, she felt so good, they were her friends, her true friends. We don't know the meaning of friendship, Ely says to me, our nights, they don't bring us together, we're all out for ourselves; she's had it up to here with having to beg to be loved, the women on the scene have nothing to give, don't ever forget it, and Ely has nothing to give either, she knows it, apart from sex, but it's all lies, she's always lying, that's something I need to know, because the truth is, she's trying to find love too. She realized in the water how alone she was – the faces had vanished and she was all alone, orphaned, not because of her mother, but orphaned from herself, that's how lost she was, she didn't even belong to herself any more. It was a man who saved her, a German on holiday in Paris. He dived in, pulled her back to the riverbank, said he was going to call an ambulance. Ely swore at him, she felt bad about that, but after all, she hadn't asked him to help her.

Remembering

I lie awake in the house in Rennes, nestled close to my sister, listening to the familiar sounds of the night. The house is a womb, a beating heart that protects and nourishes me. The clock's weights bang together, midnight strikes, I hear the cat on the gravel in the garden, my grandfather's footsteps on the wooden floor; he comes home late to avoid us, or perhaps he has to work late, but who goes to the dentist in the middle of the night, I wonder? And there's a sound coming from inside the wall that neither my sister nor my grandmother have ever heard, no one has, an electrical noise that comes up from the cellar, where the coal is kept, through the fireplace in the living room and behind the Liberty-print wallpaper – women and men hunting with their dogs, walking arm in arm, carrying their parasols, reclining beneath the branches of the weeping willow trees that droop like giant feathers over the paper people, my new friends whose stories I imagine. I feel cast adrift without my mother, the days separating us stretch to eternity. I'm four years old, too young to count them for myself, too young to have any notion of time.

I'm out at sea, swimming far from any shore.

Becoming

It's not working with Julia, we're not gelling, we're not in tune; it's my fault, my lack of experience, my obsessions too. I'm like everyone else of my generation, a product of the times, terrified of being ill, of catching something. I obsess about blood, saliva, sweat, refuse to touch the razor she leaves on the basin in the bathroom for fear of cutting myself.

I try to draw up a list of all her partners, the men and women she's been with. I ask her if she uses any form of protection, if she's been with prostitutes, drug addicts, if she's ever had a transfusion, if she's given blood in a foreign country, I'm like a mad woman, and then Julia stops me in my tracks by saying: 'Who do you take me for? You think I'm HIV positive, is that it?'

With AIDS I've found a way of wrecking my relationship with Julia from the start, and possibly any relationships I might have in the future too. I'm like my mother, I don't deserve to be carefree and light-hearted, I punish myself for being the person I am, won't let myself be happy; I make sure I stick to the family tradition, the one that says there'll be no tender romance, no happy ending, no innocent pleasure in love-making.

I write to fill the hole left by my relationship with Julia, I write from morning till night, believing in the power of my words to recreate what I have lost. I enter a parallel world hoping it will prove less treacherous, but the questions that haunt me remain unsolved.

Writing brings no comfort, it merely pours oil on the fire.

Remembering

Some French families stay behind on Algerian soil, their farms in the hands of the government. The Algerian State has taken possession of the fields and the farmland, of every tree that bears a fruit, orange trees, lemon trees, olive trees. The economy is modelled on the Soviet system, invitations are extended to the Chinese. The Chinese Circus performs in the National Theatre where my sister is dancing in *The Nutcracker* with her ballet class. The performance is being filmed by RTA and my mother has sewn green ribbons on my sister's tutu. I pick her out on the screen. I'm so proud I feel like crying as I watch her dancing en pointe, I know it's making her feet bleed.

French socialist representatives have big ideas too for Algeria, they come as guests of President Houari Boumédiène, who greets them proudly, one by one, and listens to the advice of men spurned only a few years before; people say the authorities have dumped gallons of perfume into the El Harrach river near the airport to make it smell less offensive.

The Grangaud family live in a small house across the road. I gaze at them from my window every day, watch them busying themselves in their garden, on their terrace; they spend most of their time outside, a big family that seems to keep getting bigger all the time. I'm fascinated by them.

I wonder whether they feel Algerian or French Algerian, or

Christian Algerian, or perhaps they see themselves as French people with no country, *pieds-noirs*, survivors.

They seem sad to me. I'm sad too, I don't know where I belong. I can't choose one country, one nationality, over the other, I'd feel I was betraying either my mother or my father.

Remembering

During our temporary separation from our parents, my sister asks my grandmother to sign her up for the Fête de la Jeunesse. She wants to be one of the young people parading through the streets of Rennes, she wants to be in the film they're making of the show. She's proud to be part of *la jeunesse française*, the young people of France, the nation's hope, as some say; she's proud to wear a white outfit like a tennis player's, to carry a majorette's baton, to march in step with drums and trumpets in the musicians' parade.

My sister needs the gaze of others to know she's loved, her own is not enough, and my mother's gaze comes and goes; we never know if she'll be there or not, after school, in the Thabor gardens, in my grandparents' garden; we never know if we'll ever see her again. We miss her so intensely that we have no choice but to wipe her from our memories and reinvent her in other forms, depending on how bereft we're feeling.

I watch at the kitchen window, waving a small Tricolore flag that I've made from a stick and a piece of cloth. I cheer my sister on as she parades past.

Remembering

Chinese medicine hasn't cured my mother's asthma; she follows Andréa's advice and leaves Algeria once a year to travel to Germany.

She takes a train from Frankfurt to a remote place deep in the forest to see a professor who has his own unique views on medicine, on illness. He treats his patients with concoctions whose contents he cannot divulge; my mother refers to him either as the genius or the mad scientist. I picture him with Einstein's face.

My mother spends at least a week in Germany staying at his house, which is both his laboratory and his office. Patients come from all over the world to see the professor.

The treatment consists of a series of injections. I picture my mother with tubes coming out of her body, the tubes attached to a machine that delivers a magical substance intended to open up the lungs, the bronchia and the mind. Disease is primarily a sickness of the soul, according to the professor: my mother must look into herself if she is to be cured, she must find what it is that is suffocating her.

I feel her presence everywhere in the apartment in Algiers while she's away – in her spot in the bed, in the library, on the couch in the living room, in the kitchen where I watch my father cleaning a rockfish in the sink, rolling red mullet in flour on the white tiles of the kitchen counter, making my hot chocolate; my mother's gestures borrowed by my father to reassure us, to show us he has everything under control, that he's the head of the family now, the one watching over us and setting our minds at ease: our father.

As soon as my mother returns, I avoid him. I know I'm being unfair but I can't stop myself; without her, I can't breathe – she is my oxygen, I am hers.

Knowing

After the war, my grandfather bought a house by the sea, near Saint-Malo, a ruin in need of restoration, with a large piece of land that offered endless possibilities.

Every Sunday he would go to the house and set out along the path that led to the beach, he'd pause at the top of the steps to gaze out at the expanse of nature, the cliffs, the rocks, the islands of Davier, Cézembre, the distant sea that all but covered the beach at high tide, and he knew he'd acquired much more than just a small, derelict house.

He was the owner of this space and of all the creatures that lived in it.

My mother posed for him in front of the fencing that surrounded the building works. It took a while to compose the picture, the wind was blowing her hair about. My grandfather told her: 'For goodness' sake, tie your hair back, you look an absolute disgrace.'

Thirty years later, my grandmother acquired the adjoining house. She wanted to drive out the vagrants who'd taken up residence there; she said they spread disease, they stole her hydrangea blooms, they were selling them at the market.

Remembering

Ali and I are confined to a bungalow in the Club des Pins, a resort a few kilometres from Algiers. Our parents have forbidden us to go out, we're not allowed to walk on the beach by ourselves because of the gusting wind. They've been invited to a party, we have a phone number to contact them if we need to; before they go out they make us some dinner, they have a few glasses of wine, some gin; Ali's father has just come back from a trip to Japan, he's given us both a kimono, we put them on after our showers and watch, wet-haired, as the adults get tipsy; they seem happy, I've never seen Ali's mother burst into laughter like this before.

It's spring, life is stirring, sap, power, energy, hot and sweet as the grasses that grow along the front of the bungalow and ooze a thick white liquid when I snap the blades. 'Sperm,' says Ali.

Our parents leave, we drain their glasses. It's not very much, not enough to get us drunk, just enough to make us tingle with excitement as we root around in the bungalow our parents have rented from friends, both hippy doctors, Ali says; they've hung a Mzab rug on the wall, they have incense, amber, hanging plants, paper flowers. We find a pack of cards, play poker for money. I win, Ali can't lie – I can read his mind. He gives himself away before he shows his hand, gets annoyed at himself, at me, then he starts fidgeting, he wants to do something we're not allowed to do; the night seems endless, morning will never come, our parents will never come back. Ali is gripped by terror, boredom creates fear, he paces up and down, searching, searching, searching, but for what?

We locate a secret door cut into the wall, find a gun and some pornographic magazines that we extract from their hiding place; we flick through the pages, silently scanning the pictures, clutching the gun, passing it from hand to hand.

Remembering

In Algiers I watch football matches on television with my father when he's home; he teaches me to play in the park, shows me how to fake out the goalkeeper by hitting the ball with the side of the foot and making it go off at an angle; we practise it over and over again.

When the Fennecs win, I go out on the balcony with all the boys in our apartment block, we flash our torches one floor at a time, we set off firecrackers and throw stones. I yell at the top of my voice: 'One, two, three, *viva l'Algérie*, six, five, four, *à bas le Maroc!*'

I belong to two different worlds: my home and the one I've gatecrashed – hooligan country.

Remembering

In Ghardaïa, I slip away from our group – my mother, my sister and the friends who've come with us into the desert. I want to get lost in this city of cone-like structures; I'm not trying to put myself in danger, I just want to see how long it will take for someone to notice I've gone. I'll find out how much they love me.

Viewed from the palm grove, the houses appear as one, hewn together, a single stone block with hundreds of niches and alcoves. A labyrinth that drives people to despair.

One-eyed women hurry by, covered from head to foot, a single eye left uncovered to reveal the way ahead; they walk briskly, their bodies seeming to float in mid-air, through the maze of stone, clay, earth, sand. I imagine them gliding towards a man, who waits, crouched inside an alcove, in a secret garden.

Becoming

I catch sight of Nour coming out of Julia's building. She hasn't been answering my messages. I've come to check, to see if my suspicions have any substance.

I'm in the street. Nour is walking towards the Institut du Monde Arabe; I watch from a distance of a couple of metres so I can slip behind a tree if she turns round. I could so easily reach out and touch her hair, the back of her neck – if I sped up a little I'd be able to take her by the shoulder, feel her skin. I can't tell whether I'm driven by desire or by the urge to hit her. I keep my distance.

I still don't know who Julia is, but I miss her. She's sparked something in me. I feel bereft, but being gay is more than a passing experience, it's my destiny, I must continue to live it.

At the Institut, Nour opens a door with a magnetic ID card and disappears. It's an entrance not open to the public. I stand by the door. I don't know what I'm hoping for. My life seems to be on hold.

From the top floor of the Institut, Nour looks down at me.

Remembering

There's a pile of leaves at the end of the garden in Rennes – leaves, dried grass, faded flowers. I go there every afternoon, when I come back from nursery. The mound sinks beneath my weight. I'm fascinated by what I find under the leaves – insects with antennae and pincers, worms devouring one another; I picture a body rotting beneath the compost, a man or a woman that my grandfather has disposed of during the night.

Without my mother's presence, death becomes absorbed into the land of the living, woven into the fabric of the solid world around me, the house, its bedrooms, its attic, its cellar, and into the world beyond my reach – light, the sky, clouds.

I'm frightened in Rennes, but I don't know why. The only thing I can think of is my father's absence, the fact that I never hear his voice on the phone; I'm scared my grandfather has done away with him, taken his revenge on my father for stealing his daughter.

Remembering

In Algeria, in the early 1990s, people start receiving warnings through the post – men, women, believers and non-believers alike, regardless of their politics: 'We are coming to cut your throat.'

No one who receives one of these letters lodges a complaint, for fear of bringing bad luck.

People choose to remain silent, to protect themselves, they throw the letters in the trash, letters that arrive at least once a week, bearing no stamp, slipped through the letterbox in the dead of night or in the early hours as the birds begin their chorus that seems to herald the end of the world for Algeria.

Other people receive miniature coffins; they send them on to old enemies, creditors, mistresses who've been unfaithful.

Knowing

After my sister was born in August 1962, my father left Rennes to go to Algiers and look for an apartment. My mother's family said he'd never come back, that he'd fled, that he was shirking his responsibilities.

My mother was sick from exhaustion; her father decided to have her hospitalized for a sleep cure. She had no say in the matter.

My sister stayed with one of my aunts, or with our grandparents, it's all very vague, no one likes to talk about it. One aunt apparently grew so attached to my sister she wanted to keep her, she thought of her as her own daughter, 'cuckoo syndrome', they call it; there's something poetic about it, the idea of incubating someone else's egg, but there was a much darker side to it too, the situation was a cause of great pain to my mother, pain and shame.

She kept trying to contact my father. She imagined him in the streets of Algiers, making the most of his country's newfound freedom; perhaps it had gone to his head, perhaps he too felt suddenly free, perhaps he didn't want to come back. He was Algerian, better that he should live among Algerians, leave the French to the French.

She had it all wrong.

My father was taking his time. He had a feeling that something wasn't right. His country was free, but it was slipping from his grasp. As he walked the noisy city streets, he heard young boys shouting, not in French but in English, 'Algeria Free'. He feared for his love, for his wife.

When he came back to Rennes he said to my mother: 'We could always stay here.'

But she wanted to go, to get as far away as she could from her parents.

Becoming

I call Julia at all hours of the day; she doesn't answer. I don't leave a message, but I stay on the line until the tape clicks, filling up the space on her answering machine so no one else can get hold of her.

I call her at night to wake her up, I know she's not alone. I picture her tying up her lover and photographing her as she climaxes.

I spend all evening in bed, plotting my revenge even though I have nothing to avenge myself of. The worst of it is that I'm heartbroken over a love affair that never materialized. I'm like one of the American psychopaths in the biographies I read, men who fantasize about having sex with the girls they murder.

Whenever my relationship with Julia comes up, I lengthen the time span, adding extra days to make it into a love story, to flesh it out, give substance to the affair, to balance the scales (we've never made love), to make up for what I lack (I feel dizzy without her).

I fantasize about what I no longer have, what I've never had.

I feel I've missed my chance, that this will be the story of my life, that I will always be swimming upstream, against the current of love.

Remembering

Ali prays with all his might to grow up as quickly as possible and find out what it feels like to be inside a woman. He pities me because I'll never experience this, and because it must be painful for a girl to be penetrated by a boy.

Pleasure is something more subtle in my opinion; love itself or the love we feel for another person can be orgasmic. When I say this to him, his response is: 'My mother's right, you really are crazy.'

Later, on Rue Saint-Charles, I find photos from my primary school years. Ali is always beside me, in the front row, sitting cross-legged, one or other of us holding the sign with the name of the class.

Ali chose me on the first day of school, we were twins from the very beginning, joined at the hip. And then one day we became enemies.

I look for a clue in our childhood photos, some indication of what is to come. I can't find it. Ali is always beside me, smiling. I tear up the photos and, with them, the memory of him – to me, he is dead.

Becoming

I leave music on Julia's answerphone, to scare her. The sound-track from *Powaqqatsi*, the film about how humankind lays waste to nature and ends up destroying itself in the process.

I see it as a metaphor for my love life: it's all my fault, I've ruined everything.

Remembering

June 1972. My mother comes to Rennes to fetch us, we have to pack, we don't have much time, trains don't wait for latecomers – be quick, my darling girls, I've missed you so much, my lovely girls, my dearest loves, hurry, we're going back to your father, back to our old life, hurry, we can forget all of this, it was only a few months, life is long after all, and you were fine here, weren't you, with the garden, the cat, the dog, hurry now, we're leaving right this moment, say goodbye, adieu perhaps, we may come back or we may not, that's the way it is, nothing ventured nothing gained, hurry, it's now or never, there's a long journey ahead, with a surprise waiting for you, hurry, we're going back, my darlings, back to our country, we're going home to Algeria.

Remembering

June 1982. At 118 Rue Saint-Charles, my mother says she wants to talk to me, nothing serious, but it's very important: we're going to move. I want to stay in Paris, I've made new friends, I like this town, I know I'll find what I'm looking for here. I can't afford to waste any time, I don't want to leave *my* town, I finally feel French – I don't want to lose all this, I don't want to go backwards, lose track of myself, go back to all my old ghosts. I start to cry. The song playing on the radio is Pierre Perret, 'Don't you worry, little one, it's just life, *c'est la vie*', I'm facing my mother in the living room of our small flat that we'll soon have to leave for Zurich. My mother is in tears too, but she's crying in response to the song, which, I don't realize, is about a rape.

Becoming

Ely calls me at five in the morning. 'I don't know how to say this. I don't know if there are words for something like this. I feel so alone, I'm cold, I'm so very cold. Laurence is dead. She jumped from the sixth floor. We'd gone out, she was the same as usual, no worse, I mean. She'd taken something but she seemed okay. Lizz is at the police station. They're questioning her. She was in the bath. Laurence said she could fly. Lizz didn't say anything, she thought it was just another of Laurence's crazy ideas. Not anything serious. And then she jumped. Can you imagine? She wanted to fly. Lizz called the emergency services right away, and then a police car showed up. I think the police are always involved when someone commits suicide, because that's what it is, it's suicide, it's not an accident. I feel terrible. I need to keep talking. I'm frightened. I feel like she's here, everywhere, in my flat, inside me, you know? I can hear her voice now, while I'm talking to you. She's talking over me. She's coming to take her revenge, I can feel it, but I never did anything to her, you will tell them, won't you, that I didn't do anything to her? Promise me.'

Remembering

Ever since the airport in Algiers they've been inseparable.

Ali and Tarek.

He was invited at the last minute, we still had room. His mother is the pharmacist, a friend of Ali's mother. Everyone knows her. Everyone likes her. Everyone knows her son is difficult. No one realizes how dangerous her situation is.

People say he tried to rape a girl, his neighbour, but no one really knows so people don't believe it. The pharmacist says the desert will be good for her son, she's very grateful; I'm not.

He hates women; his mother doesn't understand. She feels guilty, she left her husband when Tarek was little, she'd had enough of his lies. He lives between Algiers and Rome, he never invites his son to Italy, it's his life, he's a free agent. Tarek is left alone in the house, he's bored, he has trouble making friends, close friends, the kind you keep. His relationships are highly charged: first it's all passion, then it's hate. Tarek is violent, with her too.

She blames herself, she doesn't spend enough time with him because of the pharmacy she inherited from her father, she works too much. Tarek imagines things, imagines her with men, he's jealous; he's got it in for her, calls her a hypocrite; it's impossible, to put all *that* behind her, at her age.

To Ali's mother she says: 'My son is jealous of his own fantasies.'

Tarek wears a cowboy hat, has muscular thighs, shoulders too; he wears a skin-tight polo shirt with stripes, he has a big mouth, facial hair already, a broken nose; he has a coarse kind of beauty, rather rough, like a boxer, and he looks older than he is. Ali likes that, being with a man, talking men's talk.

I want to be Tarek.

They laugh together, he uses words like 'cock', 'bitch', 'son of a whore'; it turns Ali on. I know it does. It would turn me on if I were Tarek's sidekick.

I can't compete with him. My mother takes my arm, places her hand on my shoulder. I hate it, I don't want her protection. I'm not a victim, I'm not innocent. Friendship takes on a new meaning.

At the check-in desk Ali says: 'I want to sit next to Tarek on the plane.' He doesn't talk to me any more, he's at war with me. I don't feel angry, just sad, rejected; they're a pair, I'm by myself, I'm not capable of fighting – my girl's body against their explosive strength. I don't want to be the cinders after the fire. I'd rather be the hot coals.

In the plane, sitting behind me, they keep kicking the back of my seat. When I turn round, they say: 'What are you looking at, faggot?' I doodle, lines leading to more lines, circles, hearts exploding from the inside.

A cloud of sand descends on Tamanrasset; I look out of the window at the Sahara. I'm losing Ali.

Henri and Paola, who often travel with us, have always wanted a daughter. I've spent years rejecting their tenderness – I have parents already. This time, I go along with it, because of Ali. They take my hand, put their arms round me, kiss my face, my neck, my hair, they eat me up, they say I smell so good, I'm so like them, there's a room for me in their house whenever I want it, they have a full set of *Blueberry* comics, my favourite, and they have a fireplace, they'll build a fire at Christmas, we'll go into the Forêt de Baïnem and get some holly and a tree, daughter, my daughter, our daughter, you can't deny it, we miss you, we don't see enough of you, we'll never see enough of you.

They're sweet. My mother watches them with me, loans me to them. I use them. I have no scruples.

I'm all alone in the hotel in Tamanrasset. I'm alone in the Jasmine Gardens, alone in the palm grove, alone in the hotel lounges. I'm alone in the corridors we walk along to get to our rooms.

Ali never comes near me, never looks at me.

He gives me a lesson in betrayal. My turn will come to be the betrayer.

My mother takes a picture of me on the plateau of Assekrem. In the photo, the mountains loom behind me. The peaks are ghostly, hallucinatory – but not as menacing as the look on my face.

I'm raging, raging against myself, I'm nothing but a faggot.

They stop talking when I come near them, they don't speak to me when I ask to tag along with them, they get up and sit somewhere else when I join them at our campsite. The desert isn't big enough. I don't ask again.

My childhood is coming to an end, disappearing into a long, dark tunnel.

We're so far from Algiers, above Tamanrasset, in the foothills of the Hoggar Mountains. Everything seems possible but things are already closing in.

I'm losing Ali.

The mountains form a plateau. They are locked in a battle with the sky.

At the Père de Foucauld refuge, Henri and Paola's son, Giovanni, starts a stone-throwing fight. Tarek chooses the stone with the sharpest point and cuts Ali's head open. Ali doesn't cry even though his head is bleeding. He's changed.

They lay him down on a small army camp bed; one of the Fathers from the refuge applies a compress with disinfectant. Ali's head hurts, his mother is furious with him. I don't go to see him.

In the communal bedroom we all go to sleep harbouring secrets. I can hear the Fathers praying before they set off at daybreak for the nearest village. They tend the sick, offer help, teach children to read and write. They wear dark-coloured robes and sandals, with a cross around their necks; I'd like one too, to protect me from unhappiness.

Once in a while my sister says: 'You'll end up just like them.' She's understood – that I'm solitary by nature, that I'm at home in my solitude.

We move on from the Assekrem plateau to the desert sands. Tarek and Ali walk one behind the other, I walk ahead beside our guide. I look straight ahead, the future is all that matters.

I hear them laughing behind my back. Like the hyenas kept at bay by the fire at night – I am that fire.

We're in a chapel in the desert, watched over by Vietnamese nuns. There are four of them; I call them the 'apparitions', we don't know their real names. They come down from the refuge at dawn and go back at night without ever getting lost. They say God lights their way and watches over them. I believe them, bow my head in respect; I find them so beautiful, so holy, I'd happily kneel before them.

We take our shoes off before entering the holy place. The sand and the walls are cold. Light floods the building but I can't make out a single opening.

Father de Foucauld left writings; the nuns who guard this temple of words give them to us as offerings. I take them, to cure me of Ali – my disease, my patient.

I know nothing of God, but I create him, or perhaps he creates me, here, among these women, with words that are mine alone: I want to mend my heart.

This is the Sahara. Vast beyond all measure. This is no longer the earth, no longer the universe. This is no longer life. No longer life as I know it. This is a higher life. This is light. This is life after the light.

Tarek refuses to set foot in the chapel.

Becoming

That evening, Fred the West Indian comes home with me, but she doesn't come in. I don't offer and she hasn't asked. She's in her fifties, she's not interested in the 'young things', but she loves to talk, words are her passion. We stay outside, down in the street, talking mostly about love. Her advice is that I should forget Julia, I'm wasting my time, my energy, I should save my tears for the here and now, not waste them on regretting the past. But for me, Julia represents something different, and that's why I'm so fixated: my nights at the Kat, my clandestine existence in the city, my youth heading in a different direction from other people's. I can't quite get there, I haven't accepted who I am. It's hard work being different, even though I can't be any other way. I've taken the first step, I'm proud of myself, but I'm holding a grudge against the whole world. It's hard being gay, people don't realize, they don't understand what it actually means, the violence; I don't say how scared I am about Laurence's death, I can't, it doesn't seem right, but I have nightmares too, like Ely does. She comes to me in the night and I feel guilty as well. I haven't called Lizz, I've never really liked her that much. Ely says the hardest thing for Lizz is the suspicion cast on her, but the police enquiry has put her in the clear. Fred tells me I should find another woman, any woman, even if it's only a one-night stand, to erase Julia's memory. She also says that what she likes best about being with women is that when she's around them she feels like a man. Especially with Martine, she's so tiny, so delicate, she goes along with everything, nothing is off-limits with them; this is what freedom really means, never feeling like you're being judged, and when she's *inside* Martine, she knows she's at one with her real self, she's not lying to herself any more.

Knowing

The oddest thing about Monsieur B., my mother says, is that she didn't understand what it was he wanted, what he was looking for. She thought he was ridiculous, like that, in that state.

She remembers having asked him what exactly it was that he wanted, what he was hoping for.

He didn't know, but he felt happy at that moment, and happiness is something you can't explain.

It's not a milestone, it's just part of her life, there's absolutely no connection between Monsieur B. and my mother's body, between that man and us; she can't speak for her sisters, she doesn't know whether they're like her, without a past, living in the moment, or whether they're in denial, it all depends on how you choose to look at your childhood.

We are the parents of our lies and our forgettings.

Being

I meet Nathalie R. at the Kat; she follows me as I'm leaving, gives me her number, makes me promise I'll call her. I take the cloakroom ticket with her phone number on it, promise I'll call. She doesn't believe me, she's convinced I won't call, but at least she'll have tried, she says, she's not proud. I'm touched by this, I don't know why, I'm usually the weak one and I hate it. That's not what life is all about, real life is feelings, emotions, relationships between equals, it's not about who's stronger or weaker. I leave, I phone her, we meet a few hours later at the Deux Magots. I'm worried I won't recognize her, that she won't recognize me. The cafe is a bubble, a bubble in the city, a bubble in the world in general, it's real and it's not real. She's wearing a skirt and a leather jacket; I love her hands, the ring she wears. I look down at the ground when she talks to me, not out of shyness, or embarrassment, but because I'm keyed up. I don't know who she is, but I don't need to know, because I know who I am, I love who I am with her. I want to go with her, I'm not afraid any more, and that makes me nervous too. I've changed, I want to know everything, understand everything, try everything, I've got nothing to lose – I want to have it all, take it all. She lives in Impasse Passy, I can spend the night with her if I want, she wants me to, she really does. I tell myself I have no choice, I have to go along with her, trust her, I have to live this experience, for one short moment or forever, it doesn't matter how long, a few minutes or a few hours – pleasure is all that counts. Maybe it won't just be for one night, maybe there will be days too, lovelier, sweeter. You have to give this a go, even though it could be the wrong thing to do; she could be making a mistake, I could be making a mistake, but you'll never know if you don't try, sink or swim. She pays the bill, guides me out; I follow her lead, listen to what she says, her hand on my neck, her leather jacket beneath my fingers. You can't think too much about things in life, you'll miss your chance if you do, your dreams will never come true. She's had her eye on me for a long time, she shouldn't say it, but now that she's spilling it all out, that's the way she is, she goes for it, too bad if she falls over, makes mistakes, puts her foot in it. She was surprised to see a girl so young in a place like this, she liked it, she likes it, says it shows courage – I must be brave, or else very self-assured, either way she doesn't care, but there was something touching about the sight of me, sitting there at the bar, all alone, waiting for a hand to reach out to me. She never saw it as sad, quite the opposite, what's sad is not taking risks. She drives a dark-blue Fiat 500, her hand on my thigh. Paris is a foreign land, my land, I see flowers and dunes, I see the ocean, the cliffs, I see the stones in Place de la Concorde, the water cascading, I smell perfume, sense the speed of the car on the bends, feel the wind half slapping, half caressing my face when I wind the window down. I am air and metal, tarmac and oxygen, I am a slave to my desire, willingly enslaved. In her bedroom, dawn is already breaking, clouds casting shadows on the walls. I am at the centre of the world, I am king, queen, I am my own bride, my flesh on her flesh, my skin on her skin, her breath, her silences, her smell suffused with mine. I am with her and she is with me, she is in me and I am in her, we are as one. Everything falls away, the sounds of the city stirring, the lilac hues of the dawn sky, the wind beneath the roof, the weight of the unknown. I am the same but I've changed, I've let go, I'm floating free on this waking dream, desired and desiring – I have no past, no future, no witness, here in her hands I could cease to be, and yet I am reborn.

Being

I write the spaces and the silences, the unseen and unheard. I write the paths not taken, the forgotten roads. I hold fast to Others, those whose past flows into mine, like rivers spilling into the sea. I give voice to ghosts to stop them from haunting me. I write because of my mother, who clasped her books to her breast like children.

Remembering

When my mother comes to Rennes to take us back to Algiers, my grandmother gives me a photograph before we leave: Mardi Gras, I'm dressed as a clown, in my pink dressing gown and a pointed hat; my sister is a flamenco dancer, her hair up in a bun, castanets in one hand, a fan in the other; my grandmother is wearing her white fox-fur hat with a veil, she's happy – it's a holiday, a holy day. She played the piano and we all sang the Toreador song together. There's confetti everywhere, streamers and balloons, and we're opening our bags of treats from Monsieur B. and his wife who've come over specially for the party.

Being

We're seated around the dance floor at the Kat, the drag artists are doing their act, the backing tape crackles, it's all fake, all so real: women watching men dressed as women, men singing and dancing, wanting to stop being men for a night, for this big night. We are no longer the stars of the show, the divas, the actresses, now we are the audience, we watch, searching for the truth behind the masks; you can't change who you are by dressing up in drag, by covering your eyes, secrets can't be hidden by silence; daylight shines through the blanket of night, darkness lingers in daylight, everything turns, intermingles, lays bare truths and counter-truths, fits together and pulls apart, words are birds flying free. There will never be enough hours to embrace the truth, we shall never know who we are, what we want and expect, there are so many fruits on the tree and so many flowers in the field. Men in drag can change their clothes, put on different hats, but we are who we are, hearts and minds, flesh and blood, women together and alone; the parties, lights, tears and shadow plays will go on, the pain of being unable to probe the hearts of people we love, of people who love us, will endure, there will always be the mystery of the unknown; we shall never find the roots, the earth, the sources of our happiness and our sorrow; we can be sure of one thing only – we go on hoping.

I cross to the other bank of the Seine, a long way from my neighbourhood. The river is my guide, I don't know where it will lead me. Rivers, like time itself, have the power to propel us towards a menacing future.

In the crowd, I wonder about the way we construct our lives. What is the raw material of our stories? What is the past we inherit? Why do we choose one path over another? How do we know when we are making a mistake?

Like the figures in the cave paintings in Tassili n'Ajjer, armed with bows and arrows, we fight and resist and then lie down to rest in peace beneath the weeping trees.

There will always be war and reconciliation.

Our hearts will always hold on to the memory of our passions lost and regained.

We will always sense the presence of those we are yet to meet, those we are destined to love more than ourselves.

When the future fills us with dread, we will remember that others have embarked upon that future before us and may be waiting for us there.

The rivers may carry us along, sweeping away our past on the tide, but we cannot go back to their source. We must go forward, not knowing what lies ahead, how many loves, how many rejections, how many words left unsaid.

Thrown into the maelstrom of the city, pulled this way and that by forces we cannot see, men and women alike, the same and different, we will never stop wanting to know.